GW00471272

BROKEN STONES

by Brian Ervine

Brian Ervine (signature)

A first collection of short stories from this well-known local author, activist and singer/songwriter; evoking the people and places of a Belfast we can all recognise.

DEDICATION

This book is dedicated to my son Andrew

With many thanks toGillian Hughes for
typing and practical advice
and
Carmel Duggen for 'proof reading' and 'wise counsel'

Charcoal Illustrations by artist Yvette Pascalle Dalgarno

© Copyright Brian Ervine 2023
First published November 2023
ISBN: 978-1-8381889-9-3

Published by Cedric Wilson
Printed by GPS Colour, Belfast

CONTENTS

CHAPTER ONE

Have you seen my Daddy?

The wind was unruly and boisterous bringing a dubious promise of rain. It gusted round gable ends and whistled over chimney tops; soughed through trees and drove dancing leaves along the roadway, accompanied by various pieces of litter. Not a cold wind, but a wilful one with an obdurate mind of its own, like a huge beast that has slipped its leash.

I was walking along the Beersbridge Road, past Bloomfield Avenue. The old redbrick building that had been the Owen O'Cork mill loomed stoically on my right-hand side. I mistakenly believed it took its name from its owner until disabused by a local historian who took great delight in casting light on my ignorance. "No, it's Abhainn an Choirce, the River of the Oats." Centuries before, the locals brought their produce to be milled there.

It was too dark to see the picturesque Conn O'Neill bridge, reckoned to be the oldest edifice in Belfast, dating back to the 16th century, but, just between gusts, I could hear the rush and gurgle of violent water to my left as I approached Elmgrove Primary School where the road bends.

To my right, a narrow walkway gradually undulated towards the Avoniel Leisure Centre, following the Connswater River on its journey to meet the Lagan, and flow into Belfast Lough. I could see the towering yellow illuminated cranes in the distance straddle the huge drydock; iconic symbols of a renowned shipbuilding industry now virtually gone.

I hardly noticed him standing at the corner of the street.

I could hear his voice call softly defying the anger of the wind and myriad droplets of rain it flung violently against a shop window.

"Excuse me please!"

It was a soft thin voice, just discernible, and it drew my attention to a small figure under the yellow lamplight.

"Excuse me!" he repeated plaintively. "Please, can you help me?" He seemed a pathetic soul and at his wits' end.

He was a handsome young man. He had fair hair tousled by the wind. His blue eyes ringed with shadow were set in a well-proportioned face.

I stopped and looked around guardedly. This was a tough area, and I had no wish to be ambushed by others who may have been nearby.

Cautiously I moved towards him. His hands were empty at his side. "What's the problem mate?" I asked.

He was dressed in an old combat jacket. The zip was unfastened and it hung open. He wore a red and white shirt and a pair of washed-out denim jeans. "Have you seen my daddy?" he pleaded. "I'm worried about him. I've searched everywhere but I can't find him." He looked so mournful.

It seemed strange that this young man, I guessed his age to be around twenty-six years, should call his father Daddy as a small child would.

"Is he ill?" I queried, thinking that maybe his father was suffering from dementia and had wandered off.

"Have you seen him? He's small and stocky with a full red face and dark hair streaked with grey. His eyes are so sad."

"Like your own." I observed.

The wind gusted round a gable end, and played momentarily with an empty can that clattered across the pavement and onto the road.

"I need to find him. It's been so long." He looked so forlorn and melancholy.

"Have you been home? Is he not there?" I suggested hopefully.

"It's not there anymore. It's gone," he answered.

"But where do you live?"

My words were snatched away by a violent gust that shook a window shutter. I realised it was raining harder and dark lowering clouds scudded across the crescent moon in the black sky. The stars were gone.

"Have you been to the police?" I persisted.

"I talk to them but they ignore me."

"This guy is strange," I mused. "Maybe he's mentally ill or homeless or both; an escapee from Knockbreda Mental Institution, a few miles away nestling in the Castlereagh Hills."

"If you want, I'll take you to the barracks." I offered. I was at a loss what to say or do.

He looked over my shoulder further up the road. "Did you hear that?" He was intense. He had become animated. "Someone called my name. Did you not hear it?"

There was such hope in his face. His eyes flashed for the first time. I did not wish to dash his hope.

"No mate. Sorry." I apologised.

"You must have heard it. A voice calling my name." He insisted.

"Sorry mate."

"It's my daddy. I know it's my daddy. Oh, it's been so long. I've been so desolate; so cold; so alone. It's my daddy. I know it's him. I must go to him. I must go."

I was distracted. A car lit up the road, rain dancing in its headlights. I turned back again. He was gone.

I looked at the empty doorway where he had stood; his eyes pleading, imploring. There was something overwhelmingly sorrowful about him, as if he bore an infinitely crushing burden.

I looked about but could not find him. It was a strange encounter indeed. As I began walking home through the wind and rain, a police patrol car pulled up alongside me. The passenger side window glided down.

"Everything alright sir? You're out late?"

"Yes officer, on my way home. I was visiting friends in Martinez Avenue."

"OK sir, just checking."

"By the way. I was just talking to a young man who was in great distress. His father had disappeared and he seemed desperate to find him. The young fella may be mentally ill. Maybe you could check it out?"

"That's the third report tonight. Small, fair haired, pale, sad expression?"

"Yes, that's him."

"We'll have another look for him. He's probably a local who lives nearby. OK sir, goodnight."

The incident with the young man disturbed me. I could hardly sleep that night. Those deep suffering melancholy eyes haunted me. I dozed fitfully until the alarm heralded the resurrection of another day.

I found it hard to concentrate for the next few days in the Community Advice Office where I worked. I mainly dealt with poor souls; the demoralised unemployed; people with disabilities; the addicts and the generally afflicted, whose benefits were reduced for virtually any excuse by a government hell-bent on clawing back what little they had. "Have you seen my daddy?" The quiet pleading voice that could still be heard in spite of the storm, obsessed me.

I walked back that way on a number of occasions. I thought I might meet him, but in vain. There was no sign and I returned home disappointed.

"A penny for them!" The exclamation broke the spell of my reverie.

"What?"

"A penny for your thoughts dreamy. Your young men shall see visions and your old men shall dream dreams."

"Not so much of the old men. I'm a visionary not a dreamer!" I looked at her beautiful face smiling at me over the steaming mug of creamy coffee. "Sorry kid. Just thinking about something that happened a few weeks ago. The memory won't leave me." I told her my story.

"I should have done more to help the guy. He was like a helpless waif, storm-tossed and not comforted, vulnerable and alone. He seemed to suddenly disappear like a dead leaf borne away on that violent brawling wind."

"Oh, we are becoming poetic, aren't we?" she bantered

"It just seemed so uncanny."

"Well maybe he was a ghost; an unquiet spirit who suffered some unspeakable trauma."

"Well, whatever he was, he certainly disturbed me."

"It reminds me of the story of Hamlet's father haunting the battlements of Elsinore demanding revenge," she quipped dramatically. "Or the three weird sisters who met MacBeth and Banquo on the heath."

"Get your black cat out of here Esmerelda!"

"Grow up Gandalf. Away and trim your beard"

We laughed together enjoying the playful banter borne of deep mutual affection. It lightened my mood and I bathed in the warmth of this beautiful young woman who sat across the small table from me, amid the clink and clatter of crockery and the incessant murmuring of multiple conversations in the quaint little coffee shop.

Later we strolled through Belfast city centre. The sun had gone down. An illuminated Belfast City Hall shone like a wedding cake amid the relaxed business of the rejuvenated capital. Belfast was Lazarus back from the dead. I recalled the security gates, the indiscriminate bombings, the conditioned reflex action of raising your arms to be searched umpteen times a day. By six o' clock the city had become a wasteland, haunted by fear, derelict and forsaken. The City Hall was a white marble mausoleum. Now crowds thronged the streets to enjoy the late-night shopping a few months before Christmas. People from all over the world gave a cosmopolitan ethos to a once provincial city obsessed with its internal divisions; sectarian brutality and a most sordid little war without honour or glory. The multicultural faces and languages from Poland, Africa, Hungary, Syria and Lebanon lent cultural diversity and excitement to the place. The future seemed bright. We no longer counted our dead and wounded, or waited in trepidation for the next news bulletin.

The days passed amid the prosaic humdrum of normal life. For this, most of us were grateful after decades of moral darkness when murder stalked the city streets and country lanes.

Again, I found myself walking home in the early hours from a soirée at a friend's house in the Bloomfield area. Again, a storm had engulfed the British Isles as the warm wet westerly winds battered the Irish shoreline. The scene was Shakespearean, "madman's weather" – a sign of dissonance in the universe when graves opened and the dead walked.

The wind howled mournfully through the big trees in Cyprus Avenue. The autumn leaves, animated by the wind, spun across the avenue and pirouetted in the air. An array of various unionist flags battled in frenzied protest against the violent onslaught of the elements. It was a macabre dance of death accompanied by clattering tin cans and the distant boom of plastic dustbins in back entries.

I was a little tipsy. My friend had a source who supplied poteen on the cheap. He had poured some onto a teaspoon and lit it with a lighter. It burned with a blue flame.

"Good stuff eh! Get it down ye boy! Got it from north Antrim. There's a lemonade man who delivers it in Ballymena."

I had just passed Elmgrove Primary School and was walking in the direction of Clara Street when I thought I heard someone calling me. The wind was whipping cigarette packets and papers violently against a brick wall. There it was again. Unmistakable this time. "Have you seen my son? Lad? Have you seen my wee boy?"

He was a man in his late sixties, small, stocky, dark haired streaked with grey. His face was ruddy and his blue eyes were desperate and pleading. He wore a plain white shirt, and dark trousers held up by braces which I noticed under a brown unbuttoned jacket. "Have you seen my Danny? Oh, that I could find him! Oh, that I could find him!" he keened.

Even in my semi-inebriated state I saw that he bore a resemblance to the young man of my first uncanny encounter. I was not afraid. The wind wailed and moaned over rooftops.

"I think I saw him about six weeks ago just up the road there." I pointed back up the road. "He was looking for you."

It began to rain heavily as he pushed past me in the direction of the bridge over the Connswater River.

"Oh, I hear him. I hear him! I can see him! Danny! Danny! Thank you! Thank you!" he called over his shoulder to me, and then he was gone, as if dissolved in the ether like the witches in MacBeth. Gone.

I blinked and rubbed my eyes. Was I dreaming? I walked home to my bed where I dozed uneasily 'til dawn.

"Why do you think this is all happening to you then?" her lovely eyes twinkled with good natured mockery. "Do you think you're psychic? A bridge between dimensions?"

"I need a physic not a psychic. All this is giving me the sh..."

"Collywobbles!" she speedily interjected.

"Call it whatever you want but it's really weird. I mean, nothing like this has ever happened to me before. I remember when I was eight or nine, sneaking into the Castle Cinema on the Castlereagh Road, and watching 'The Pit and the Pendulum'. It frightened the daylights out of me. I had mum and dad up nearly all night. I was too terrified to go to sleep. Now I can read Edgar Allen Poe without flinching."

"Are you sure it wasn't that poteen you drank that caused you to imagine restless spirits from beyond?"

We were sitting in the quad at Queen's University. Noise here was muffled among the cloisters of the campus. It was an oasis of calm amidst the growling snarl and mumble of fleets of traffic, and the frenetic movement of people on their way home from offices, building sites and schools. Here was a quiet haven of serenity and peace.

I had 'phoned her that morning and arranged to meet her after her lectures. The clock on the wall read four thirty pm. I noticed V.R.1848 set into the red brickwork harking back to the reign of Queen Victoria when Ireland had been united. The day would not last long, and would give way to a dusky gloaming. Light splashed on the paved quad from windows, and a faint mist caressed the lamps softly, almost sensually.

"It's almost biblical!" she declared.

"What do you mean?"

"Well, you have Abraham and Isaac; Jacob and Joseph; David and Absalom; and of course, the Almighty Father and the Eternal Son."

"If you believe in all that. Look, I just don't know what to make of it. It's really beginning to irk me."

The quad began to bustle as students crossed and recrossed it, arms full of books, or bags slung over their shoulders. The ethnic mix showed the progress that the country had made since the cessation of hostilities.

A very young couple with their little toddler son passed by. The father carefully shepherded the little fellow as he made his unsteady way forward. Then the boy, quite spontaneously, took off at a tangent, bolting for freedom, pursued by dad who stopped him, grabbed his arms and steered him back in the right direction. His gleeful giggles, pure running laughter of infant delight flowed through the air.

"There goes a very dangerous person. The wee guy with the Donald Duck bib!" I pointed with mock horror.

"Ahhh he's just a wee dote, a great wee soul."

"The original sin is hanging out of him. Mark my words." I joked. "Come on and I'll buy you something to eat in Botanic Avenue. Oh, we'll be eating al fresco by the way!"

"Oh, al fresco. Very la di da."

"Don't get excited. It's a fish supper in your hand." I smiled.

"Oh, you old romantic you. How can a girl not succumb to your irresistible charms?"

There in the twilight, I took her in my arms and kissed her gently. We held each other close for a few moments and walked through the gloaming, suspended between day and night, as the earth slowly turned again towards the dark.

"Well Mr McKeown, that's it! I'll send in those forms to the Appeals Tribunal right away. I reckon your case will be dealt with at the end of this month. I'll represent you."

"That's great son. You're doing a great job. I don't know what I'd do without you. When them forms come through the letterbox it puts the wind right up me. I can't see very well, you know?" We were in my office in the Advice Service on the Newtownards Road. Across the desk from me was a man in his seventies. His clothes were ragged and crumpled, and gave off the whiff of tobacco, alcohol and grime. Grey hair surmounted a battered lived-in face, the result of a tough life of suffering and self-neglect. His children had emigrated to Australia and Canada, and his wife had died ten years before. I had heard from different sources that Mr McKeown was known as 'Arsenic' and he'd been banned from every pub in East Belfast. "He'd start a row in in an empty house," one man wryly commented.

"I'll just 'roll up' before I leave." He took out a plastic pouch of cigarette tobacco from the side pocket of his jacket, followed by cigarette papers and began to expertly roll a cigarette.

"You're from the Beersbridge Road aren't you?" I asked.

"Born and bred in Grove Street East," he answered, and proceeded to fastidiously lick the sticky edge of the flimsy paper held between the fingers of both large wrinkled hands. "I joined the Army when I was sixteen, I made sergeant twice and lost my stripes twice." He shook his head regretfully. "Fightin' and drink, Dr Jekyll and Mr Hyde. That was me. Always mouthin' when I should have been listening." His nose and scarred face certainly bore silent testimony to his words. "I married a lovely wee girl. Didn't treat her right. Didn't treat my family right. Later I did some jail time here – the ole Troubles ye know. I was a resident in Her Majesty's Hotel Long Kesh for a wee while." His dark eyes twinkled with innate humour.

"Can you remember anything that happened involving a father and his son in that area?" I urged.

"Well, a lot o' things happened, rioting, gun-running, assassinations, feuds." He was in a reverie, looking over my shoulder, back down the long vista of years. His past, with its joys, tears, bloodshed and pain. "Well, there was a wee lad called Danny Boyd. Must be forty years ago."

The hair rose on the back of my neck and I experienced a tingling shiver running down my spine.

"There was a feud between the two main unionist paramilitaries. Wee Danny was a van helper. His driver was a Commander of a particular organisation. He wasn't a bad guy either. Ye know ye get good men trapped in bad circumstances – like flies stuck in jam. Some of them were better men than the law who were hunting them, if ye know what I mean."

"So, what happened to them?" I asked impatiently.

"Well, a squad of men from the rival organisation abducted them both on the Shankill. Wee Danny wasn't in anything. He just happened to be there. They took them to a lonely spot, on Island Magee near the Gobbins and held them there. Then their killer showed up. His nickname was The Spiv, well, so the papers said, and ye can't believe them ye know – gutter press. I remember....."

"Yes," I interrupted, "what happened then?"

"Well, the gang assured Wee Danny that he would be alright. They only wanted the Commander."

In my mind the scene unfolded, the lonely seascape, the smell of salt on the wind, the wonderful beauty of creation in contradiction to the obscenity that men were about to commit; the terror and the fear, the pleading, the constant sound of waves on a distant shore. Two victims, on their knees, hands tied behind their back, the warm tears trickling down the young man's pale and drawn face. The silent desperate prayers.

Then came their executioner, dressed respectably in a neat suit and tie to avoid suspicion, seemingly a reputable pillar of the community; someone whose presence would reassure us there was nothing to fear. Aside maybe a debate, "Shall we kill the kid?" "We have to. He can identify us." The comforting hand on the young man's quivering shoulder, "Don't worry, you'll soon be walking with your daddy son."

"Anyway. They killed them there. Their bodies were found six months later in a shallow grave. A squad from Antrim were rounded up and charged. But ye see Danny's Da, ye called him Danny too, stood every night at the top of the street waiting for him to come home. Ye'd see him there in all weathers, even into the wee hours of the morning. His wife died o' heart trouble when Danny Junior was a baby. He was an only child. All they had was each other.

After the funeral he just faded away, the shell of a man. He couldn't cope with the weight of the grief on his poor shoulders. Broken hearted he died only a few months after."

"That is so awful," I mumbled, not really knowing what to say.

"Now I'm not a religious man, an old reprobate like me, but you'd like to think that it wasn't the end of the two of them, wouldn't you?"

"Oh yes indeed." I humoured the old boy.

"Well, I'll be on my way round to the East Belfast Mission to get my dinner. It's cheap and it saves me cookin'. Could ye hand me that walking stick?"

I opened the door for him as he slowly tapped out of the office.

"Oh here, don't forget your cap." I handed him his duncher, the once iconic symbol of working-class Belfast.

"I need it. There's woodpeckers about," he smiled. "All the best son and thanks again."

In spite of myself, I felt the tears well up in my eyes as I closed the door on the old man's back.

"What a desperate sad story!" she exclaimed. "But why did they murder the young man? It seems so pointless."

"They were after the Commander. Danny just happened to be there. What do the Yanks call it after a bombing leaves scores of civilians dead? Collateral damage. He was in the wrong place at the wrong time, like so many poor souls in our own senseless little war."

The day glowed warm and cheerful. A mild westerly wind from the Atlantic playfully teased the coppery red and yellow leaves strewn along the roads and pavements of the treelined avenue. Animated, they rustled gleefully like the fairy folk in a chaotic sunlit 'hooley'.

"This really is a glorious day, "she smiled. The sun filtered through the gaily swaying branches and dappled the leaf strewn pavements.

In the blue-sky white clouds scudded like galleons bound for exploration and adventure. High up in the heady freedom of the heavens, two white gulls circled and whirled, calling to each other in the golden light. Then they joined and soared together up towards the orange disc of the warm autumn sun.

"Look," she pointed. "There goes Danny and his Daddy. It's a sign that they've found each other."

We traced their flight into the sun, united they vanished from sight.

"I'd like to think so," I sighed. Putting my arm around her shoulder we strolled slowly together through the mellow light.

CHAPTER TWO

The Stuff of Murder

D avy was a taker. He had been humbly born in a two up two down, outside toilet house with a backyard. He was one of ten siblings. His hardworking and harassed mother had been driven to an early grave by constant childbearing, and the violent abuse of a drunken husband. He had learned to refuse nothing except insults and blows.

His father, a shipyard labourer, was old school, and considered his wife to be a chattel to produce offspring and look after the overcrowded home, in one of the interminable backstreets built hastily to house the workers who poured into Belfast at the end of the nineteenth century to feed the growing Titan of industry that gradually hardened and dehumanised people.

Money was scarce, especially those weeks when his father lost a lot at the bookies, or went on a reckless, sometimes violent binge. Then his mother scratched and scrimped and borrowed; the pawnshop on the main road a last desperate resort.

He remembered well his hand in his big sister's as they made their way stealthily to the pawnbroker, his sister tried to avoid being seen as she smuggled a clock or a shirt or jewellery through the side door only to find a number of neighbours on the premises, as abashed as she was.

His father, resentful and angry at his lot, would regularly terrorise the household, liberally doling out brutal beatings to his wife and children, especially Davy.

He attended a tough inner-city secondary school where survival depended on submissive acquiescence or the ability to scrap. Davy had been buffeted at home by the fists of his father, so fighting in school was not a big deal, and he became adept at it. He had a quiet inoffensive younger brother in a lower form, so Davy had to intervene on many occasions when Mark was bullied. He was intelligent, but never really achieved academically. Owing to his father's influence, the one good thing he had done for him, Davy was employed as an electrician.

They met in the lift of a high-rise block of flats on the outskirts of east Belfast. She had her blonde hair tied in a bun and looked neat and dapper in her nurse's uniform. A little on the plain side, nevertheless she had a certain matronly attraction that appealed to him immediately. She would have been in her mid to late thirties, short and slightly on the plump side.

He was just under six foot tall, in his mid-twenties, powerfully built with dark features and a lived-in face that bore the scars of many gutter fights and bar-room brawls. He was in his working clothes, a dark blue boiler-suit, and carried a toolbox.

"What floor?" she enquired.

"Twelfth thanks," he warmly replied.

"I live on the thirteenth. I haven't seen you here before," she smiled.

"I just moved in last week."

"Oh, with your wife?"

"No, I'm not married, I'm too young," he joked.

A warm sense of relief soothed her, though her facial expression did not change.

"I'm single too. An unclaimed treasure my mum says."

The lift had been silently ascending.

"Pleased to meet you..." he lifted his eyebrows.

"Flora," she proffered her hand.

"I'm David. Call me Davy." He took her hand in his and gently shook it. Strangely they were alone, even at this time when people were travelling home from work. "Could this be Providence?" they both thought.

The lift stopped at the twelfth floor and the doors opened with a hydraulic sigh.

"Well, all the best Flora. Hope to see you again."

"You bet you will," she determined. "Great to meet you Davy. God bless!"

She entered her flat. It was clean as a whistle and sparkled; everything in its place and a place for everything. She thanked the

Lord she had a good job, a comfortable home and a caring Christian Fellowship, but she was so alone. The loneliness was like a disease, a space that spoiled a beautiful painting, an unwanted ghost that haunted her existence.

She had been born into a loving family in the middle-class suburbs, had attended grammar school, then on to university where she easily graduated in nursing with distinction. There followed a successful career and achievements. Still she yearned for a companion, an intimate loving relationship resulting in children.

She was a midwife and had seen many miracles of birth. "Oh Lord. What about me?" she prayed. "What about me? Have you forgotten to be gracious to me?"

She remembered the interview she had had with her pastor.

"Maybe the Lord has given you the gift of celibacy," he suggested.

"Oh, I hope not," she thought, but kept her own counsel. "Easy for you to talk with your wife and five kids."

She had forced a smile when she politely wished him goodbye at the door, after he had completed his visit with a sincere prayer that the Lord was in control and was working all things out according to his will. On closing the door, she had forcefully thrown a cushion to the floor and kicked it violently for half a minute around the living room. What she growled through clenched teeth would have made the elders pale and wide-eyed with incredulity.

They met on the lift a few mornings later. Her heart leapt as Davy entered. His face lit up when he saw her and he drew close so as not to be overheard by several other passengers.

"Good to see you again Flora. How's it going?" he asked effusively.

"Fine Davy. Where do you work?"

"On building sites mainly. I'm a self-employed spark. Served my time in the yard, then branched out. I'm working in Holywood at present."

"I'm in the Ulster Hospital for my sins. That's where the Lord has put me."

"So, you're a Christian then," Davy enthused.

"Oh yes. Saved when I was a child."

"What Fellowship do you go to?"

"The Earlswood Presbyterian Church. And you?"

"The Wesleyan Methodist. I'm actually training to be a local preacher, then hopefully into the Ministry."

"Isn't that wonderful."

By this time the lift was almost full, having stopped at nearly every floor on the way down. They had been squeezed up against each other in a back corner of the elevator; an experience deeply pleasurable to them both, although they probably wouldn't have admitted it, even to themselves.

At last it stopped in the middle of the foyer.

"How are you getting to work?" asked Davy.

"Oh, I walk onto the Upper Newtownards Road and then take the bus to the Ulster."

"Sure I can drop you off at the Ulster, drive on to Dundonald village, and go to Holywood by way of Craigantlet."

"Ah I don't want to take you out of your way Davy."

"It's not as if you're leading me from the paths of righteousness now is it," joked Davy. "It's no problem."

"Well, if you're sure," she succumbed.

"This way." He led her to an old grey banger, parked outside the towering high-rise.

"Jump in." he ordered cheerily. "And watch out for the mice!" he quipped, as she settled in the passenger seat with a glowing smile.

"I throw a cat in when the mice multiply," he jested.

It was a lovely crisp Spring morning and the car sped through the sunlight. He drove her out of the estate on to the Sandown Road. He then took a right onto the Upper Newtownards Road. The traffic wasn't too heavy country wards, but it was very heavy as cars from the outskirts, dormitory towns of Newtownards and Comber, grumbled their way towards the city.

"Look at that," he pointed, "gridlock. To think cars were invented to quicken travel. It all seems a bit pointless."

"You're so right Davy," agreed Flora, "you're so right."

He stopped the car at the Ulster Hospital.

"Thank you so much Davy. You're a star. One good turn deserves another. I'll make us a wonderful dinner at the weekend. Now not another word. You're a real gentleman."

"OK Flora. God bless. Have a good day!"

He drove through Dundonald village. The name always reminded him of Disney's famous duck. He smiled, and took a left onto the Carrowreagh Road. The old car laboured up the steep slope until it reached the brow of the hill. He pulled the car into the left. This was such a wonderful place. Dundonald was shining in the vernal sunlight, spread out before him like an enchanted fairy tale village. Above Ballybeen, far in the distance, the gloomy Mourne Mountains dreamed in the mist.

He was surrounded by the drumlin hills of County Down, and to his right he could discern the imposing dark folly of Scrabo Tower, built as a monument to a bygone landowner desperate for immortality. It stood as a perpetual silent sentinel atop of an escarpment that guarded

Strangford Lough, and dominated the skyline for miles around.

The lough had been named centuries earlier by the Norsemen as they encountered the strong current of the lough Fjord. He could imagine the Dragon ships propelled by men at oars to the beat of a primal drum, skimming over the water to pillage, and violently throw down the glory of Nendrum and other monastic settlements.

Ahead, and slightly to his left, the water of Belfast Lough gleamed under a cloud scattered, windblown blue sky. He thanked God he was alive and felt a joy and awe arise within him as he was confronted by the panoramic sweep of majesty and glory.

It wasn't always that way. Only a few years before he felt alienated from creation, from self, from others, from everything. Burdened by the immensity of his own existence, weighed down by the silent desperation of having to cope and find a meaning for it all. Then the change came.

He was awakened abruptly from his reverie when a car roared by at speed. "Thank you, Lord," he shouted at the welcoming sky and jumped into his car. He drove over Craigantlet and down by Whinney Hill. Belfast Lough rose up to meet him. Then he turned left onto the carriageway and left into the Holywood worksite.

They met again a few days later. She had just entered the building when he was about to leave.

"Hiya Davy," she beamed.

"Haven't seen you for a while."

"Oh, I'm on shifts this week. Are you missing me then?"

"Just wondered," he mumbled matter of factly.

"I haven't forgotten about that dinner I promised you," she reminded him.

"Don't worry I'd have done the same for anybody," he lied.

"Well it wasn't anybody, it was me. Thank you again for the lift. Are ye out for the night?"

"I'm going to a prayer meeting and Bible study. We have house groups in the church. It starts about eight o' clock."

"Are you free Saturday night?" she queried.

"Well, I think so." He began to feel slightly embarrassed.

"Well, it's dinner for two in my place. It's one floor above you. The thirteenth. Let's hope it's lucky for some," she laughed. She was about to enter the lift.

"What time?" he asked.

"Say around eight. Now be there. No excuses. Bye bye!"

The doors closed on her, and Davy, flattered by the attention and the offer of a meal went happily on to his Bible study. He found her attractive in a maternal and matronly way, reminiscent of the mother who had been taken from him as a child and it exacerbated his desolation, rejection and loneliness.

She was off work the following Saturday and bought in all the provisions for the meal that evening. She had met that jumped up patronising bitch Stephanie Crean in Sainsburys at the Holywood Exchange, who took great delight in rubbing her nose in the fact that she wasn't married. She had waited for the inevitable question.

"Well now Flora, have ye got a man yet?"

Flora shook her head.

"You'll have to get a move on. We all have our sell by date you know."

"You had yours years ago you malicious bitch," thought Flora. "You must have drugged the poor eejit on the wedding day. Anyway, you were the only one he could get. He makes the Elephant Man look like James Garner."

But of course, she never said this although she really yearned to. Instead, she politely asked "How are the children Stephanie?"

"Well Tristan has just started his first year of uni. He's studying medicine you know. Anastasia is doing three A levels. Such a clever girl. And young Geoffrey sits his GCSE exams this summer. They're all doing very well. Thank you. Well maybe we'll bump into each other sometime again. Goodbye dear."

"Goodbye Stephanie. God bless." Flora forced a smile, concealed her clenched teeth. "You hateful old cat. You were a lousy boring Nurse Tutor," she mumbled out of earshot.

"What was that you said dear?" enquired Stephanie.

"Oh, just all the best. Bye bye."

She spent hours cooking the meal. After putting a clean cloth on the table, she laid gleaming cutlery for two and just kept her eyes on the leg of lamb slowly roasting in the oven. Her apartment was cosy, warm and nurturing. 'A perfect love nest' she told herself.

Davy had to work that Saturday morning on a site off the Shore Road. He was busy wiring up an extension when the plasterer and his helper entered.

"Well, if it isn't Divine Davy, emissary of the gods." the helper sneered.

Davy's heart sank. He was standing on a step ladder and stretching up to adjust some flex.

"OK Johno. How are you?" Davy sighed. Before his conversion to Christianity Davy and Johno were, let's say acquaintances. The term friends didn't really apply. They had attended the same secondary school and lived in the same area.

Johno was a wisecracking loudmouth and Davy, one night under the lamplight in the gloaming of a Ballymacarrett back street, had given Johno the hiding of his life. After that Johno was quiet as a mouse in Davy's presence.

Then he heard of Davy's Christianity and the wisecracking started again. "Get yer donkey out of here!" "Hey can you turn this water into wine?" "He'd rather shag a Bible than a woman."

It wasn't the warm harmless friendly banter that came from tough builders or shipyard workers. This was sneery and malicious, calculated to demean and humiliate, usually in front of an audience.

"I hear you're still thumping that Bible," mocked Johno.

"You're lucky he's not thumping you Johno!" commented the plasterer with a grin. "Go and mix some stuff and let's get on with it."

They worked steadily for a few hours with Johno making a sneering supercilious comment every time he came near Davy. Then as Davy was packing up his tools to leave, Johno quipped "What about that retard of a brother of yours Davy. Is he still slobbering at the mouth?"

Davy grabbed him by the throat. It was as quick as lightening. Johno turned pale and started to gurgle.

"A wee word in your ear Johno. I want to tell you that the Lord has used you to teach me a wonderful lesson today."

Johno gurgled "Aaaggh."

"The Lord has taught me what a great protector and restrainer he is. Are you paying attention?"

Johno gurgled "Aaaggh."

"Well, He's protecting you and He's restraining me. Nod if you understand. That's why you're not eating through a straw in the Ulster Hospital today. Now put up or shut up."

He released Johno with a push.

"Agh, agh. Sorry. I was only joking Davy. You're supposed to be a Christian."

"Christ would have saved you. I'm not Jesus. I'm Davy."

"Sorry mate. It won't happen again."

"Church militant on earth, eh mate," winked the plasterer.

She completed the finishing touches of the table layout as the time interminably crept to eight pm. The cutlery gleamed golden under the candlelight. She arranged the napkins just so. Was she being too pretentious, too pushy? She remembered what her friend had told her, "Don't turn up on your first date in a wedding dress. Don't appear too keen. You'll drive the victim off. Slowly slowly catchee monkey." Oh she was just a laugh. Very worldly though. She certainly had been around a few corners and had much experience in dealing with the opposite sex.

Then she recalled the Brethren guy. He was so maddening. So naïve. Initially he really came on strong and when she quite naturally responded, he backed off. He said "No, no, no", but his body was shouting "Yes, yes, yes." His subconscious messages were completely garbled.

"He shouldn't have done that to any girl never mind me. It was really mean of him to call the police and have me removed from his flat. There really was no need for it. I would have gone peacefully. Then to have an exclusion order slapped on me was utterly ridiculous. He even reported me to the Kirk Session of my church. And that clucking passive hen of a mother of his turned into a screaming Harpy. She should have called him Oedipus, not Samuel. It would have been more fitting. Mammy's little angel."

Her train of thought was abruptly derailed by the dingdong of a singsong doorbell. She made a mental note "Change that bell. It really is too much."

There he stood, tall, masculine, rugged and handsome, weathered on a hundred building sites. He was wearing tight fitting black cord trousers and a beautiful blue shirt that accentuated his powerful physique. The two top buttons of his shirt were undone hinting at the hairiness of his chest under his tough weather-beaten face with its smiling mouth and twinkling dark eyes. In one hand he bore a small posy of miscellaneous flowers and in the other two large bottles of beer.

"I hope you don't mind the alcohol," he held up the beer apologetically.

"Of course not," she soothed. "Come in, come in."

"My goodness" he thought, "she cleans up well."

Her blonde hair, usually tied up, cascaded around her shoulders. Her blue eyes were limpid pools he could swim in. She had applied the makeup prudently 'accentuating the positive and eliminating the negative' to paraphrase the old song. Her wide red mouth was inviting and voluptuous; her teeth even and white.

She wore a light turquoise loose-fitting top and a dark skirt that ended above the knee and accentuated her femininity. Her dark stockings adding to her desirability.

Davy, to put it proverbially, was 'gobsmacked'. His eyes widened with incredulity at the transformation of this rather pleasant looking girl into a beautiful sophisticated woman that set his blood on fire.

"You you look g-great," he stuttered.

"And you don't look so bad yourself," she returned. "Sit down in the armchair near the fire and I'll pour you some beer. We can have a drink before we start. I'll put the wine on the table now. I wasn't sure what your attitude to alcohol is."

"Some people are always whining about grape juice," Davy joked. She smiled, but looked somewhat blank.

"Wine – whine – whining – grape juice. Some of the fellowships say the wine that Jesus drank was unfermented grape juice. Do you get it now?" he asked hopefully.

"Oh yes, the penny's dropped. That's very clever Davy."

He was delighted as a puppy that has had its tummy rubbed.

"That's one of my own," he boasted.

"You're very intelligent," she encouraged.

Davy was hungry. He had eaten very little that day in anticipation of this meal, and he was not disappointed. She had pulled out all the stops and spared no expense.

Cream of chicken soup for starters was followed by lamb shank, creamed and roast potatoes, asparagus tips and peas and cabbage with a beautiful gravy. Dessert was a melt in your mouth apple crumble with cream and custard. Tea, cheese and biscuits followed. All was interspersed by generous libations of red wine.

She was the perfect hostess who saw to her guest's every whim. He was a little embarrassed, but flattered. No-one had ever paid him this much attention in his life.

He had been hungry and was now satisfied, but another insistent hunger had manifested when he saw her, grew as he smelt her perfume as she came near to serve him at the table.

"I'll help with the washing up," he suggested.

"You will not indeed. I'll not hear of it. You're my guest. Here, sit on the sofa and I'll get you another glass of wine."

Background music had been playing all through the meal, not loud enough to spoil the conversation about jobs and friends and different Fellowships. As he sat on the sofa, he became euphoric, contented. She joined him, and sat close.

"This is like heaven," he mused. "I've never felt so content."

"That's a great compliment," she replied. He kissed her gently and she responded.

Let's draw the curtain there. Exploration of undiscovered, forbidden worlds and feelings took place, bliss and self-revelation.

Although they did not technically leave the path of righteousness, it could be stated that it was a divine miracle that they did not fall off the edge to tumble into the dark abyss. They left each other that night tousled, breathless and full of passion, as yet unrequited.

Both tossed and turned disquietly in their own beds. He was torn by the warmth of affection and the dark passion that he could barely withhold, and that may be visited with divine chastisement. She was pleased with the company, and warm light shone into a lonely cheerless existence. "At long last," she thought, "I have a man."

The sermon the following morning was "If a man think that he stand, let him take heed lest he fall, but his Master is able to make him stand." Of course, the minister illustrated the text with biblical references to King David and his nefarious affair with Bathsheba; and to Samson, God's delinquent, "a he man with a she weakness".

Davy was squirming in his pew all the way through, yet even then he could not get Flora out of his mind; her perfume, her female shape, her touch, the soft curving contours of her body, the taste of her lips. Still, he made a resolution to strangle the relationship in its infancy before it grew like Baron Frankenstein's monster to destroy him and all his ambitions.

When he saw her again the next Monday in the foyer as he returned home from work, all his resolve dissipated like smoke before the wind.

"I hope you enjoyed the dinner on Saturday," she beamed.

"Oh, it was great. I'll have to return the favour some time."

"That's not necessary."

"Maybe we could go to a movie next Saturday." He could feel the great overwhelming desire like a great hunger welling up inside him, making his body react in a way that embarrassed him. He became flustered.

"I would love to Davy." She kissed him on the cheek. "Thanks for the offer."

So, the relationship developed. He was careful to avoid being too much alone with Flora. He was frightened of himself and how things might end up. She made herself useful. She wanted him to be dependent upon her; to see her as valuable, even indispensable to him.

"Davy, it's pointless me cooking just for one. Sure I can drop you down a dinner in the evening when I'm not working shifts in the hospital."

"It doesn't matter love, that's too much trouble."

"It's no trouble at all Davy. It's a pleasure."

They went for a drive down to Helen's Bay one summer evening. They walked the coastal path at Grey Point where the gun emplacements guarded the approaches to Belfast Lough during the Second World War. The sun was slowly setting over the lough, and stained the sea blood red.

Walking hand in hand through a copse of trees, he paused and kissed her passionately. She responded in kind, and so they were bound in a passionate mutual breathlessness until they were interrupted, first by a friendly shaggy dog who gave the alarm that his master was on his way. They hurriedly broke from one another and laughed joyously.

On the way home they bought some fish and chips in Holywood and ate them on the esplanade, as the last rays of the dying sun drained away behind Cave Hill and Black Mountain.

"Look Davy, why don't I do some washing and cleaning for you? I have a huge washing machine. It'll be no trouble to pop your stuff in there and 'Hey Presto' it's done."

"That would be imposing on your generosity Flora," he protested half-heartedly.

"Well, if I'm going to clean your place as well, I'll need a key Davy."

It was Davy's twenty ninth birthday, so they decided to go out to dinner together to celebrate. He had booked a table for two in a classy little restaurant in Bangor.

"This is a lovely spot," noted Flora as the first course arrived. Soup for her, ribs for him.

"Yeah, I like Bangor. It's dripping history. Comgall founded a monastery here. Do you know he had three thousand monks studying the scriptures here? It was the missionary training centre for the ancient Celtic church."

"So that's where the tradition of the World-Wide Missionary Convention comes from, that they hold every year, "smiled Flora.

"Columbanus sailed from Bangor with thirteen others to take the gospel to Europe. The Roman Empire was crumbling and Europe was about to fall into an era of barbarism. The monks lit lamps of learning and civilisation in a growing moral darkness," lectured Davy enthusiastically.

"You seem to know a lot about it. It's all new to me," admired Flora.

"It's part of a church history course I'm taking in my local preacher's course," he continued "It shows what a wonderful Christian heritage Ireland has. It used to be called the Isle of Saints and Scholars."

"A pity it's not like that now. Belfast is the Holy City of pubs and churches. If they don't get filled with one type of spirit, they get filled with another," she joked. "They even speak in other tongues. My brother is fluent in Mandarin after a skinful." They both laughed. "How did you become a Christian?" she asked, focussing her big blue eyes on his ruggedly handsome face.

"Well, a few years ago I met this guy I'd known growing up. He explained the gospel to me. I was suffering from depression; a lot of it rubbish and unresolved conflicts and wounds from the past. There didn't seem to be any meaning to my broken and wasted life. I turned to the Lord and knew peace and acceptance, probably for the first time ever. I'd a reputation for scrapping, drinking you know. That all stopped. The Lord didn't just give me a new start, He gave me a new life to start with. Anyway, that's the short version of my story," he broke off apologetically.

"Oh, that's wonderful," she cried. "I wish I had a testimony like that. I grew up in a Christian home. I can't ever remember not believing."

"It takes the same grace to save a moral churchgoer as it does to save a drinker or an adulterer."

They were interrupted by the arrival of the main course. "The beef is absolutely delicious here," he enthused.

"I'll stick to the salmon."

"Would you like some wine with your meal?" he asked.

"I'm not drinking if you're not, I'm satisfied with tea."

"I'm driving you see."

"I know, I admire you for it," she reached over and squeezed his hand.

Later that night they entered Flora's flat. "Sit down and I'll get you a drink. Something special for your birthday." After lighting a sole lamp and some candles, she entered the kitchen and emerged with a small glass in one hand and a bottle of amber spirit in the other.

"Here, try that," she commanded good-humouredly. He sipped the dark brown liquid.

"Whoah, whiskey, but it's sweet."

"Southern Comfort," she informed him. Then she went to the mantelpiece and took a small box beautifully wrapped. "Happy Birthday." She bent over and kissed him generously on the lips.

He had noticed her beautiful new dress earlier with its plunging neckline which accentuated her cleavage, a mysterious valley full of forbidden treasure.

"Oh, thank you Flora. What is it?"

"Open it and see."

He quickly ripped off the paper and opened the ornate cardboard box to reveal a glittering and expensive watch. "Oh Flora, that's too much."

"Nothing's too much for you Davy, nothing."

After a number of drinks, the alarm bells sounded in his head. This is folly. This is not on, but the overwhelming compulsion gripped him.

When they had embraced and kissed for a short time, she rose from the sofa and held out her hand. He took it. She gently pulled him onto his feet and led him into the bedroom. He was not so much led by Flora as compelled by overwhelming desire, a ravenous hunger that needed to be fed.

On the building site the next morning he agonised over the events of the previous night. "What have you done Davy? "What have you done?" Having gone to bed with a voluptuous Greek goddess, he awakened beside a plain little woman who snored. Some enchantment had beguiled him. Maybe Flora was a witch!

Guilt was a persistent tormentor reminding him of every detail of his moral abandonment, recalling pleasure mixed with the scalding sorrow of remorse. Horror was an unwelcome interloper in the pit of his stomach.

"Are you all right son?" asked a friendly joiner. "Is anything worrying you? It's just you've been staring into space for the past ten minutes."

"No, I'm alright, thanks mate. Just a bit tired. Had a late-night last night."

He tried to lose himself in his work, but still the incessant images could not be expelled from his mind. The volcano had erupted and the dam breached. He was full of dread. Would the inevitable nemesis descend upon him? Would the Sword of Damocles fall in divine retribution upon his head? "Oh Lord I am so sorry," he prayed, but got no relief.

Then a terrible thought pierced his heart like a flaming arrow from the bow of the Evil One himself. "What if Flora gets pregnant?"

The scenes formed before his eyes. The whispering in the Fellowship. The furtive looks and muffled gossip. A wedding, standing next to Flora, her distended belly hardly covered by the loose wedding dress. He would be morally obliged to marry her. Oh God, no. What about the lay preacher's course? What about ministry?

"Knocking off time lad," the big joiner had put his hand on Davy's shoulder. He started.

"Easy son easy. Are you sure there's nothing troubling you?"

"I'm fine Sam. Nothing that a good night's sleep won't remedy," he lied.

"See you in the morning then. All the best."

"Yes Sam, thanks."

He had joked with Sam only the other day "The carpenter from Nazareth is looking for joiners." He felt like a real low life hypocrite. He gathered his tools into his box and walked to his car.

He smelt the delicious odour of cooked food as he opened the door of his flat.

"Is that you Davy? Wash up and I'll put the dinner out for you. It's a special treat."

"Flora, you shouldn't!" he protested.

"Nonsense. I was on an early shift today". She wore the same light turquoise shirt and the dark skirt as when they first had dinner together. She looked good, and in spite of himself he felt the stirring of the awakening monster within.

"Flora, about last night," he began.

"It was wonderful Davy. Thank you so much. How was it for you?"

"Ahh, ahh g-great," he spluttered, not wishing to smother her obvious happiness. "What a coward you are," he reproached himself.

After a meal of lamb chops, potatoes and vegetables consumed by candlelight in the warm ambience of the cosy room, aided and abetted by three measures of Southern Comfort and a designer beer, all his resolution dissolved like the witches in MacBeth into the mist. He was easily diverted from the rocky path of righteousness into the dark and gloomy shadows of Purgatory Wood.

So the relationship continued..........

She was becoming indispensable to him and he more and more depended on her. She catered for his every need and saw herself as his future wife. While he still harboured moral scruples about the whole affair, he decided to drift along with the gently flowing current of circumstances. He enjoyed her body, but did not love her. When she declared a week after their first intimate liaison that it was 'that time of the month', he literally and metaphorically breathed a deep sigh of relief and liberation.

He rationalised his behaviour by telling himself it was only a temporary dalliance. "It could have happened to a bishop." Indeed, it had happened to a fair number! He blamed Flora for everything, rather like Adam in the Garden of Eden when he excused himself and shifted the guilt to Eve for the Fall.

Still, he was uncomfortable and uneasy in the depths of himself, especially in church and in prayer meetings. He was convicted by his conscience, especially when the minister seemed to individually address him in his sermons. "Who is the greatest detective in the world," he had preached. "Not Sherlock Holmes or Poirot. It's your sin. The Bible states 'Be sure your sin will find you out'!"

There he was, the congregation's 'blue-eyed boy', soon to be a local preacher, and then into the ministry of the church. He was a working-class lad from the brawling backstreets of Belfast soon to become a leader in Christ's Church. "If only they knew," he moaned. "If only they knew."

While calling on his brother Mark, who still lived in the family house, he visited the outside loo in the backyard. As he sat, door open, his brother's red Staffordshire Bull Terrier emerged into the yard carrying, with great difficulty, a bone nearly as big as his head. He was looking for a place to bury it. Davy became fascinated as the dog, Barney, attempted to conceal this treasure. Confronted by only tiles and concrete, Barney placed the bone in the middle of a channel a foot wide that guided water from an outlet pipe from the sink to a square drain with a grating over it. He then nudged tealeaves around the base of the bone which rose like the rock of Gibraltar. Barney was not satisfied, so he manoeuvred a hand shovel that stood against the back wall, and daintily placed it over the bone. It was patently obvious that the bone was still clearly visible. Davy had laughed at the time. 'He who covers his bone shall not prosper' parodying a Bible proverb, 'He who covers his sin shall not prosper'. Barney seemed pleased, snorted in triumph and kicked back both legs respectively before waddling back into the house, a job well done. The prophetic symbolism was certainly not lost on him.

Davy's anomalous situation began to distress him. His conscience plagued and persistently condemned him for his hypocritical double life especially after Bible study or a worship service.

"Is something troubling you Davy?" asked the minister one evening. "You don't seem yourself. Would you like to speak to me?"

"No Rev Moore, I'm fine, "he lied. How could he come clean? Oh, how he wanted to talk to someone.

He tried to broach the subject of their immoral lifestyle with Flora on a number of occasions.

"Flora, we can't go on like this. I'm living a double life. It's displeasing to the Almighty."

"You're too hard on yourself Davy. Sure everybody's living together now. We're not doing anybody any harm. It's the way of the world."

"That's the problem. It's the way of the world, not the Christian way."

She took him in her arms and cooed "Well we could tie the knot permanently."

He shuddered inside, "God forbid!" he thought.

One Saturday, Davy had no work commitments and went in to the city centre just to relax and stroll around the great metropolis that is Belfast. As he wandered along Royal Avenue towards Waterstone's bookstore, he heard his name being called "Davy, Davy! Is that you?"

He turned, and there she was, Amy, a beautiful girl from his Fellowship. She was a few years younger, small, neat, fresh and bright and smiling as she approached him.

"Sorry Amy, I must have walked past you. My mind is elsewhere. How are you?"

"Still teaching infants in a Primary School. Lovely kids but the original sin is hanging out of them. A senior colleague told me how to control them. Nail their feet to the floor and lace their milk with brandy."

She really was a lovely person. Not only physically beautiful, but a radiance seemed to emanate from deep within and caused her eyes to merrily dance and sparkle.

"Would you like a coffee?" she asked.

"Thanks, I wouldn't mind."

He spent an hour with her in a nearby café amidst the busy hubbub of customers and the clink and clatter of crockery. For a short time, he was transported from temporal existence into a transient ephemeral bubble where the misery of his circumstances dissolved. He could honestly say for the first time in months he felt happy, clean, joyous even. Wholesome was the word for this chance encounter.

When he opened the door to his flat and entered the living room, he was confronted by Flora who was poised in the middle of the place ready to pounce.

"Did you meet someone in town?" she enquired friendlily.

"Yes."

"A date I expect. Had you asked her out?"

"No. I met a girl from my Fellowship. How do you know anyway? Did you follow me?"

"I was in town and happened to see you in Royal Avenue with that girl. You were with her in that café for over an hour. What were you talking about? Have you found another mug to do your bidding?"

Flora had transformed from an outwardly balanced lady into a hate filled Harpy, a cross between Lady MacBeth and Lucretia Borgia. Davy paled with shock.

"Now listen carefully lover boy. You're my partner, nobody else's and I won't let you forget it." She approached him and put her face, contorted with malice, up to his. She poked him as she snarled

"I wonder what they would think in that Fellowship of yours if they knew you were screwing little old me on a regular basis. Oh you're great ministry material you are! Just say I turned up one Sunday morning and exposed you in front of the congregation, eh?"

"You wouldn't." he gulped.

"Oh, wouldn't I? Why don't you try me? I wonder what Miss Goody Two shoes would think?"

"It was a chance meeting."

"It better be," she threatened through bared teeth and twisted mouth. "This is the way it's going to be from now on my love. You don't bother with any women. You be home here every night unless you have a good reason. You're not going to burn and blow me out; use me as a chattel and then cast me aside. Now you think about that Romeo." Her eyes were staring in her head like someone deranged. "And I mean every word." She left, violently slamming the front door.

Davy was overwhelmed. He sat on a chair, head in his hands. "What now?" he moaned. "For God's sake, what now?"

He complied with the blackmail. For the present, the fear of being publicly exposed outweighed the burden of guilt he now bore.

Her demands were simple. No other woman would be tolerated. He was expected in most nights except for a good reason. They would sleep together and he would perform the duties of a partner.

The relationship became toxic. Resentment smouldered like a manure heap, hardly disguised by a veneer of inane pleasantries and feigned affection. After all, he had to keep her sweet.

An ugly metamorphosis had transformed Flora's personality. Her insecurity had bred a dark malignant pathological jealousy. After all, he belonged to her. He was God given. The union had been consummated. Formal ceremonies meant nothing. There was no record of Adam and Eve undergoing any man-made ritual. No, Davy was hers and no-one else's. What she had she held, with the ruthless tenacity of any great dictator.

Davy's abhorrence of Flora was now greater than his initial attraction to her. Having been drawn to her by her apparent kindness and attention, he now hated her. He had been flattered by the gift of her body. Now sex was a nauseating ordeal for him, devoid of all warmth and affection; a degrading duty and a slavish performance.

His workmates at the building site noticed the change in him, the once cheerful lad who pestered them occasionally with promises of heaven and warnings of hell. How were they to know that Davy was living in a hell of his own.

At church his friends noted his reluctance to become involved. "Something's wrong with Davy. All the spark and crackle has gone out of him. He's depressed. There's a rat gnawing at his soul."

"You're not the first to notice, I need to have a word with him."

Davy's evangelical zeal drained away like the golden light of a Cultra sunset. He could hardly read his Bible. His interest in the spiritual slowly ebbed away like a low tide. This was the Twilight of the Gods for him.

Davy found it hard to pray. God seemed to have left the receiver off the hook. His mind was plunged into a dark trough of despair. He couldn't free himself, like an antelope struggling in thick mud, or a fly caught in treacle.

He thought of the aging couple who lived two floors above him in the flats, two retired teachers, no family, no friends; both addicted to alcohol, each became a focus for the other's resentment. They vented their silent desperation in sometimes violent and bitter domestic dramas.

Then one night, as a particularly blazing argument climbed to a crescendo, the dear old lady committed the ultimate act of anger and despair against God, the world and her husband by flinging herself from the balcony of the high-rise flats. They had actualised each other's existence by inflicting pain and insult; by gradual mutual destruction. Now there was nothing. He died soon after she was buried, of a broken heart they say. His existence crumbled away like a condemned ruin. Davy was horrified, but saw a terrible portent in the whole affair.

The pastor telephoned him at work and arranged a meeting at the manse that evening. They sipped coffee in the parlour of the manse. It was an attractive room, modestly furnished, with a lived-in welcoming atmosphere.

"Well Davy, how's it going?" asked Rev Moore.

"Ach, everything's fine," replied Davy limply. How could he begin to tell this representative of the church what he was? He felt so uncomfortable, a complete hypocrite.

"You don't sound too convincing my friend. You don't seem to be yourself this weather. Are you having a crisis of faith or something like that?"

"No, no. I still believe pastor, no, no!" he leaned forward in his chair.

"You know you've got to preach a trial sermon before the congregation on Sunday morning - for your local preacher's exam." He saw the look on Davy's face. "Had you forgotten?"

"Oh yes. Sorry pastor, I've been busy. Could I not postpone it?"

"No Davy. We have a full schedule on our rota of preachers. No can do"

"Pastor, I don't think I'm cut out for the ministry."

"Nonsense Davy. We all agree the Lord's hand is upon you. Don't be getting cold feet. You'll be fine. I have every confidence in you."

"I don't think I'm up to it," stumbled Davy.

"If you thought you were I'd doubt your call. No man God used ever believed himself to be adequate."

"But…" began Davy.

"I'll hear no more of that nonsense Davy. I'll see you on Sunday morning. We're all excited to hear you." The pastor put a reassuring hand on his shoulder as he gently led him to the door.

"Davy," he smiled, looking into his eyes," I'm just a 'phone call away. If there is anything you want to discuss don't hesitate, OK?"

"OK. Thanks Pastor."

Later that night when he entered his flat, Flora was there waiting.

"Where were you tonight then?" she demanded.

"The pastor wanted to see me about a preaching engagement."

"Well, I'm in need of spiritual comfort, you can meet my needs tonight."

"Look Flora, I can't keep on living like this. It's wrong. It's so wrong."

"Well, you could change that. You could marry me, couldn't you? That would solve everything wouldn't it?"

The thought was abhorrent to him. Again, he thought of the old couple up above.

"Oh, and by the way," she held up a little black address book. "Is this yours?" she teased.

"Yes. That's private. You've no right to take that. Give it to me," he growled.

"And you've no right to take me and then cast me aside like an empty beer can. You can't have your cake and eat it."

He moved toward her and snatched it from her.

"Oh, don't worry. I've made a photocopy of all of it. I'll be 'phoning all your mates and contacts if you ditch me mate." Her tone changed, "Anyway we don't have to fight like this do we love? Sit down. I've made some sandwiches for your supper. Sit down and I'll bring in the tea."

Davy sat down, resigned to his fate. "Good God deliver me," he silently prayed. "Good God deliver me."

He never told Flora about the preaching engagement at the church on Sunday morning. Three pithy points for prospective preachers, an introduction and a conclusion. Given his lifestyle, it was a wonder that he had been able to prepare it, never mind preach.

After the introductory hymn and announcements, he was called upon to take over. He arose from his seat on the platform and approached the lectern. He declared the text and began to preach. He was gaining in confidence with every minute when he noticed Flora, suited and hatted in her Sunday best, quietly slip into a seat at the end of the pew half way down the hall.

Their eyes met. When she realised that he had seen her, she smiled at him, a smug, malignant, triumphant grin of total dominance. Horror possessed him. He imagined her leaping up amid the congregation, screaming poisonously and demanding revenge. He beheld the looks of incredulity and disappointment in the faces of his brothers and sisters, aghast and shocked.

Of course, nothing happened. This was a warning shot across the bows of the good ship Davy to keep him compliant with the wishes of his captor.

He stumbled through the rest of his sermon, non-plussed by Flora's all-pervading presence, no less horrible than Marley's ghost was to Scrooge or Banquo's bloody presence at MacBeth's feast. Pale and drawn, trembling within, he stumbled through to the last 'Amen'.

As he was making his way towards the exit, she linked his arm and accompanied him. She was sweetness itself, smiling wonderfully as she was introduced to Davy's friends. She was his nemesis disguised as his blithe girlfriend. He cringed inside as they smiled warm farewells to the members of the Fellowship, but their eyes, like Judas, betrayed them both.

"Oh David, where have you been hiding this young lady? Introduce us why don't you," enthused an elderly couple.

"This is Flora. Flora, Mr and Mrs Somersby."

"Oh, so pleased to meet you dear," clucked the elderly mother hen with the short grey hair and smart green suit. "We've been praying that our Davy might meet a nice Christian girl and settle down. What do you work at?" she asked peering over her glasses.

"I'm a nurse at the Ulster Hospital."

"Ahh a nurse," exclaimed Mrs Somersby. "No wonder nurses are called angels. They do such a wonderful job, don't they George?"

Davy died inside. This was all he needed.

"Angel from the pit of hell," he silently thought.

"Come on dear. All the best folks! Dinner is beckoning. I can smell the roast." Off they went, and so it went on. The well-meaning friendly comments and friendly banter of the congregation. Flora standing, smiling shyly, holding Davy's arm and appearing to be an unplucked bloom of sweet Christian virtue.

It was with untold relief he drove off with her from the church carpark. Davy went out later to the evening service, more to get away from Flora than with a true heart to worship. She dogged him. She had the mentality of a stalker and wanted to know his every move.

He left half way through the concluding hymn, not able to bear any queries or questions about Flora from those who had been at the morning service. What was he to do? He was in hell "where peace and rest can never dwell where hope n'er comes that comes to all."

Of course, she was waiting for him when he entered his flat.

"I've made you some supper love. I'll get it for you. Sit down and make yourself at home."

"I don't want supper. And this is MY home and you're here too often for my liking," he half whispered through clenched teeth.

"Oh, it's like that is it. Well, I'll expose you, even if I have to chain myself to the church railings," she snapped. Then she saw the look on Davy's face and changed tack. "When we're married things will be different. All this stress and tension will disappear like a morning mist."

"Married! Married! To you! Your head's cut! It would be like marrying a cross between Irma Grese and Medusa. I can't think of anything worse than marrying you. Now get the hell out of here before I throw you out. And give me the key you have to this place. Get out! You're not welcome!" The volcano had erupted and he was shocked as his scalding temper exploded.

"You're not getting rid of me that easily. After all the promises you made and the way you led me on. I'll do you, you sanctimonious creep," she screamed.

"I made you no promises. It was all in your mind woman."

"What did you expect me to believe when you had me on my back!"

"We were wrong. I'm sorry. I can't go on like this. Now give me my key."

"No way lover boy," she hissed. He spied her bag on the coffee table and lunged for it. She anticipated this, and, grabbing at the bag simultaneously, both fell on the coffee table which collapsed with an almighty crack. She was shrieking like a demented banshee, kicking like a girl on fire.

He wrenched the bag from her, disengaged from her and stood up. Taking her purse from her bag, he retrieved the key just before she leapt on him again, grabbing his hair and wrapping both legs around his middle. Her skirt was up around her waist. For all the world the scene resembled a clip from a soft porn movie. They collided with the door to the balcony which gave way before their combined weight. Her hands clung like limpets to his hair and she squealed like an infuriated Amazon in the heat of battle.

She sank her teeth into his left ear. He yelled in pain. In a split second, in the heat of battle, he had considered trying to throw her off the balcony, but the action overtook them as they staggered in a mutual death grip back into the living room. Chairs overturned, ornaments smashed until he fell on top of her onto the copious sofa, and he grabbed her with both hands round her throat. She spat a piece of ear into his face. He began to tighten his grip when, abruptly, two police officers burst into the flat.

Concerned neighbours could not imagine what was happening to that quiet big Christian fella who lived uneventfully across the way. They thought he was being beaten up, or something worse, by burglars, so they rang 999.

Following the police were Davy's pastor and two elders, whose concern for his depression and puzzling change of behaviour, had caused them to make an emergency visit to a suffering lamb of the flock. They were dumbfounded.

"Bitch!"

"Bastard!"

"Rotten hypocrite!"

"Fruitcake!"

"Sanctimonious Pharisee!"

"You're useless in bed anyway!"

"Piss off!"

The two hurled insults at each other, and Flora was able to register a final protest to Davy's nose before they were, with great difficulty, finally separated.

When the fog of war finally cleared from their eyes, they realised the presence of the police, the pastor, the elders and some of the worried neighbours, the two calmed down. Flora rushed out and to her own flat, and Davy crumpled in a heap on the sofa.

After Davy's pastor had contacted Flora's pastor; the concerned neighbours had departed bemused and whispering; the police had interviewed the two combatants, neither of whom wished to press charges, and, save for the wreckage in Davy's flat, all returned to a semblance of peace and normality. After finding the piece of his left ear that Flora had bitten off, Davy went to hospital.

Over the next few days both received counselling from members of their respective churches. Flora was soothed and calmed and received great sympathy from senior members in the Fellowship.

"Imagine that wretch taking advantage of poor vulnerable Flora," remarked Mrs McCabe to Mrs Kelly, the elder's wife.

"Shocking shenanigans," tutted Mrs Kelly. "Leading the girl on like that."

"I'm so sorry pastor," Davy apologised with tears in his eyes. "I know I've let myself and everybody down. I'm so ashamed."

"Cheer up son, it could have happened to a bishop!" commented the elderly George Gallagher "In fact it has happened to a few," he winked at Rev Moore. He had been an elder in the Fellowship for over thirty years and had ceased to be shocked at some of the predicaments and pitfalls that some of the Lord's flock wandered into.

"So, you're saying that Flora was blackmailing you for sex."

"I can't blame her completely. She said she would expose me publicly to the church and all my friends. I was so afraid of being exposed."

"That's the stuff of murder," sighed George, shaking his head.

"Indeed," said the pastor, "the stuff of murder."

A few weeks later, Flora moved out of the tower block on the advice of her counsellor, and got a comfortable flat in Dundonald near the hospital. She felt hurt and aggrieved and so disappointed that her romantic vision of a married future with Davy had come crashing down on her head.

"Anyway," she vowed, "there are plenty more men out there."

Davy was disciplined by being denied communion for twelve weeks;

completed his local preacher's course and is studying for the ministry. He is now engaged to Amy.

Flora is still doing a wonderful job of nursing in the Ulster Hospital and attends her Fellowship regularly. As far as I know, she remains "an unclaimed treasure".

CHAPTER THREE

Sweet Anti-Christ

"Why did you try to kill the baby, your own nephew?" the detective asked in exasperation. The interview room was brightly lit. A desk with two people facing each other dominated the space. Another detective stood at the door.

"I've told you before."

"Tell me again."

"He is a threat to the human race. That's why."

"How can a baby, not yet a year old, be a threat to the race?"

"Hitler and Stalin were babies too, weren't they? Weren't they?"

"Yeah, but nobody could have known how they turned out."

"Turned into, you mean. Turned into monsters. If you had knowledge about what they were to become, would you not have killed them in the cradle?"

"Nobody knew."

"But I know what my nephew will become. He'll make those two and all the other tyrants look like a schoolgirl choir."

"How could you know that? How could anyone know?"

"It's laid out in black and white in the Holy Scriptures."

"You mean your interpretation of the scriptures."

"It's clear."

"What's clear?" the detective rose and walked away from the desk. He plunged his meaty hands into his trouser pockets and sighed. He was of medium height, stocky, his head, seeming to rise straight out of his brawny shoulders, was close cropped. His eyes were dark, lined. Cynicism was written all over him. His years on the job had mentally and emotionally hardened him.

Years of checking his car for bombs, ducking and diving from place to place; of finding bodies in rubbish skips, and down back entries; of having had fellow officers murdered, maimed; had forced him to build a metaphysical wall around his psyche. Ego defence mechanisms, his shrink called them.

But this was something different. The young man before him seemed to be open, honest, law-abiding and decent. It seemed incongruous that he should have committed such an act. He came from a good Christian home. His mother and father, who were members of a local evangelical church, had been heartbroken over the incident; and while in no way excusing the enormity of his crime, had still shown, not only their disappointment but their never-ending love for him.

Here he sat, early twenties, neat, tidy and non-descript, with dirty fair hair and blue eyes. He had been enrolled for university, but decided to take a year out, and worked in a charity shop which raised money for missionary work in Africa.

The detective swung round." For Christ's sake, how could you even think about killing the child?"

"For Christ's sake I did it," replied the young man calmly.

"Take him back to his cell."

"What are we to do?" Mrs Blake addressed her husband. "Why would he do such a thing? He's always been such a good boy."

"Well, things will have to take their course dear. He must have had some sort of brainstorm," said her husband, half to himself.

"Gina and Tim are in bits. To think if Tim hadn't acted as he did the baby would be.....oh it's too horrible to contemplate. He loved Gina so much, why would he try to do that to her?" she complained.

"Maybe he was jealous of the child," surmised her husband. "She always cossetted him, fought his battles, protected him from bullies. She was more of a mother to him than you."

"Don't start that again. You know I'd been sick, in and out of that institution. It isn't my fault I'm so fragile."

"Well, he takes after you. There was always something strange about him. I couldn't put my finger on it but something unnatural."

"Well, he was tested and he was slightly on the autistic spectrum, a mild form of Asperger's."

"That doesn't explain what I mean. There was just something off kilter."

"Are you saying your own son was mad," she said defiantly.

"Look, I don't want an argument, not at this time. I love him just as much as you do. I'm just trying to find a reason."

"That mission you went to didn't help. Always talking about the Last Days and the Second Coming. Putting things into his head."

"The wee man preaches the truth. Everybody twists and distorts it for their own purposes. It's not the Bible that screws people up. They were screwed up before they read the Bible. Isn't it amazing that atheists blame the God they don't believe in for all the bad things that happen in the world? No, the wee lad's in need of psychiatric treatment. Thank God Tim stopped him in time. Maybe he's needed treatment for years and we were in denial, telling lies to ourselves."

"Oh, thank God that wee darling baby was spared. Thank God," she said.

"Thank God our wee darling boy was spared," murmured her husband.

"I knew he was a bloody nutter," exclaimed Tim, as he stood in the kitchen with a beautiful baby in his arms.

"Don't be so cruel. He's a poor broken soul."

"He's a balloon. He tried to kill our baby, remember."

"But it's so out of character," she mused as she laid the table for dinner.

"He was always a weirdo! He always seemed to resent me."

"You're imagining things."

"I am not. He always wanted your attention."

"I was like a mother to him, what with mum being ill so often. He was always so vulnerable. He had victim written all over him. Bullied at school, bullied everywhere he went. I knew he was socially awkward, but my God. Well hopefully he'll get the treatment he's always needed."

"They should lock him up and throw away the key," spat Tim, holding the baby close to him and kissing his downy head.

"Well by the grace of God he's alright, aren't you my beautiful baby boy?" She took the baby, held him above her head with two hands. Pleased and plump, the parcel chuckled, his bright blue eyes sparkling with glee.

"They can't let your brother loose Gina. We can't ever trust him again."

Gina moved towards the window and looked out at the trim green lawn at the back of the house. Everything was so ordered, neat and under cultivation; just like their lives had been until recently, when the devil had broken into paradise and spoiled their so predictable existence.

"How did it come to this," she mused, gently shaking her head. "How did it come to this? My poor brother."

She met Tim at university, both of them green and callow. Their mutual attraction had been immediate. There followed the idyllic university courtship; the halcyon days of naivety, wonder and love; varsity; then a short engagement after they had graduated. He in chemistry. She in history.

They had both enjoyed running the local church youth club, so teaching had seemed the natural option for both. After successfully completing their PGCEs, they obtained jobs in respective schools. Then marriage, a nice home with a nice mortgage on a nice house in a nice suburb. Neat and trim like the lawn she gazed at, as the low sun filtered through the branches of the trees, and dappled the garden with shimmering light: beautiful and elemental; strange and ethereal.

She thought of her vulnerable brother whom she had protected all of his life. His very presence exuded victimhood, an unconscious signal to every predator that stalked the dangerous shadows of our sophisticated society - the weasels under the cocktail cabinet; the bullies in the playground, the gangsters in the underworld, the poisonous snakes in government and politics, and the potential for evil that stalks every human heart. How could this artless individual be capable of such a thing?

"Gina! Gina!" he held up the moving bundle of babyhood who burbled and gurgled happily. "He's hungry love. His nappy needs to be changed."

He was resentful of the child even before he was born. All the fussing. He could hardly get near his sister whom he loved devotedly.

She was older than Gary, and had been a protector, advisor and guide. It was always she who had looked after him. As a child he could only remember his mother being 'sick'. Not physically, but mentally fragile, and it was always Gina who had been there to look after and feed him, while his mother had been incarcerated in various mental institutions.

It was Gina who put a stop to boys in his class bullying him. He remembered being taken by the hand to their doors and confronting his tormentors. It soon stopped. On one occasion she had waited for a particularly nasty brat. She shadowed him through the park. On a desolate spot behind a clump of bushes she thrashed him, promising more if he ever touched Gary again. He never did. But she couldn't be there all the time, and Gary, with his social awkwardness and artless demeanour, was fair game for those who get a rise from humiliating others under the camouflage of 'playful badinage'.

"The anti-Christ is about to enter the stage. If he is not walking the streets of Europe, he is about to be born to wreak havoc on mankind and the rest of the Lord's creatures. This man will manifest in himself all the characteristics of the great dictators of the past, from Nimrod the Hunter to Genghis Khan, right up to modern times, Hitler, Stalin, Pol Pot. This man, this 'Son of Perdition', will out rank them all in manipulation, diplomacy, cunning, guile and utter ruthlessness and cruelty."

The preacher on the stage like pulpit of the Zion Covenant Tabernacle was a tall handsome middle-aged man. He was dressed impeccably in a plain grey suit, with just a hint of pinstripe in it. His white shirt, with a blue tinge, was set off by a dark navy necktie. His only concession to ostentation was the twinkling of his silver tie pin; his expensive watch and the white handkerchief, sprinkled with large red polka dots, which hung recklessly from his breast pocket. What his clothes lacked in loudness was more than compensated for by his compelling voice; his utter passion for his subject and his dramatic delivery that involved his whole person which would put an Olivier or a Branagh in the shade.

The hall was basic and functional. A plain wooden cross was fixed to the wall facing the congregation. Elderly ladies with hats, men in suits, younger families in more casual wear and teenagers daring to tempt Providence, and dressed, or 'undressed' as a tutting elder would comment, in more modern garb. The audience was transfixed as the visiting dynamo paced up and down, arms and gestures accentuating the drama of his speech.

The light was fading outside the hall and the last rays of sunlight shone through the large arched windows painting a reddish yellow glow onto the platform, that momentarily was bathed in a strange otherworldly light from the window. It soon faded and was replaced by the bright lights that lit up the whole hall and shone on an eclectic mix of people, hungry for knowledge and experience from the unseen spiritual dimension of a God that most of them had embraced.

"We are in the beginning of what the Bible calls the 'End of Times'. We hear of wars and rumour of wars, an increase in earthquake activity, plague and pandemics. We see them all on the increase. These are but the birth pangs; the earth in labour, like a pregnant woman, writhing in torment before the birth of something suffering and spectacular about to be born.

But before the Lord returns, the anti-Christ must appear, Satan's counterfeit to Our Lord. He will deceive the world with his expertise in propaganda and politics, and will talk of international peace.

Then this pretender to Christ's throne will reveal his true nature, total tyranny, depraved despotism, destructive dictatorship and overwhelming oppression. The population will not be able to buy or sell or work without the mark of the beast. Could it be a barcode tattooed on your head or forehead? Could it be a microchip implanted on the back of your hand or in your head? But the son of God shall return. The sacrificed lamb shall appear as The Lion of The Tribe of Judah, and his roaring shall make the heavens and the earth tremble."

"Amen! Amen!" shouted Gary.

"The humble suffering servant shall be the Lord of Lords and King of Kings."

"Amen! Hallelujah!"

"Instead of a meek and mild servant, he shall slay the wicked with the breath of his mouth. He shall return as the Avenger of the blood of the saints."

"Amen! Amen! Praise the Lord!" Cried Gary ecstatically.

"And every knee shall bow to him. Some shall bow voluntarily in heaven. And some shall bow involuntarily in hell."

"Amen!"

"But every knee shall bow."

"Hallelujah, praise the Lord!" Gary jumped to his feet; arms upraised.

A cacophony of 'Hallelujahs', 'praise the Lords' and 'hosannas' rose like a wave from the congregation. The band came on stage, taking up their instruments, and noisily broke into the praise of Him who lives forever.

Gary heard the key noisily turn in the lock of the holding cell. He had fallen into a light sleep as he prayed, and the sound disturbed him. He rose to a sitting position on the side of the cot that served as a bed in this narrow holding cell in the police station.

"OK Blake, you have a visitor." He was whisked out of his cell by a police officer, and across the hall to the interrogation room. On entering he saw the back of his pastor's readily recognisable balding head. "All the hairs have been numbered," the pastor used to joke, rubbing the partially shining sconce." A light to lighten the Gentiles, eh Gary?" Gary smiled at the memory. He sat down on the chair opposite.

"Hello Gary, how are you keeping son?"

"Fine pastor."

"Do you need anything?"

"No thanks. I seem to have everything I need bar my freedom."

"Well let's hope you regain that soon enough." He was a large warm man with a benign face and a welcoming demeanour.

"The police came to see me, Gary. They were asking about you. What could have motivated you? They asked me if you were mad."

"Well, I'm in good company. The Lord's family thought he was mad. Demon possessed even."

"True Gary, but he never attempted to murder anyone did he?"

"I was doing mankind a favour. The child is the anti-Christ. The Lord told me to kill him." Gary became animated. "I was called by the Almighty to do the deed. I had to obey."

"Do you think our Father ordered you to murder a helpless infant?"

"He is the one who causes desolation, the destroyer from the pit. God spoke to me. He did pastor. He spoke to me."

God spoke to Gary as the sun set on Belfast Lough. He had been contemplating the wonder and glory of creation as the great red orb gradually disappeared behind the reptilian back of the hills across the water, and fired the scattered clouds with radiant glory. He imagined Valhalla, the Twilight of the Gods, Wagner's Ride of the Valkyries, and Mallory's Morte d'Arthur, with a dragon prowed Viking burial ship blazing and sailing into the incandescent west. He mused on the vast divine metaphor of the passion and death of the eternal Word made flesh. The sky was splashed with blood red light reflected in the golden chalice of the lough.

People passing; young couples holding hands; mothers pushing buggies with fat little babies with open faces and smiling toothlessly. The elderly creaking along supported by walking sticks or rollators. Men and women running energetically towards Crawfordsburn. A group of youngsters on cycles, babbling as they passed. All this did not disturb his reverie.

He basked with pleasure in the warm, gradually diminishing sunlight of the summer evening. A playful breeze caressed his face and gently ruffled his hair like an ultimate lover. He was at one with everything, a part of the rhythm and pulse of existence. He breathed in time with the universe, the tides, the winds, the trees and mountains, the ebb and flow of an immeasurable and infinite cosmic stream, the sun, moon and stars, the whirling galaxies and exploding nebulae.

His eyes swept the line of hills across the lough, Black Mountain, Divis, Knockagh with its sad dark monument in dumb commemoration of the war dead of County Antrim; Carrickfergus, to the lough mouth at Whitehead with its long pier, fragile and jutting out into the water.

The tri-gabled Royal Cultra Yacht Club painted white stood on his left with its impressive mast and yardarm planted in its front grounds, exuding the confident affluence of its well to do clientele of north Down. Its windows glowed like golden honeycomb as they caught the radiance of the departing sun. He hardly noticed a man with a camera on a tripod attempt to capture the numinous presence which lay beyond the sunset.

A little boatyard lay just ahead of him. It was filled like a little hospital with patients undergoing repair. A few hundred yards away from the shore, over a dozen little sailing boats were anchored. They bobbed rhythmically as they gently rode the slight swell of the lough's current.

The voice, "Was it a voice?", stopped him in his tracks. Could it be what the ancient Hebrews called the Bath Quoll (the daughter of the voice of God). It was clear, compulsive and overwhelming. It confirmed what he had suspected. His sister's child was the anti-Christ. The sister he loved so much. She who had loved and protected him since he was a child had given birth to the anti-Christ. That man she married; he knew from the first he was sinister. She should never have married him. He deceived her, charmed her like a hissing snake. He took her away from church, and from him. "I always knew about him. He never had me fooled," he murmured to himself.

The baby looked helpless, vulnerable, lovable even. It was the birthmark on his left shoulder that gave him away. Almost the shape of a shamrock with a short stem. It could easily be turned into 999, but also, more importantly, 666. That was the clue. He bore in his body the mark of The Beast. Of Revelation. He then resolved to kill his infant nephew. The only question was, how could he accomplish his divine mission?

"And the rest is history," the pastor interrupted. "Did you never think you could have been wrong Gary?"

"I was under orders. I heard the voice. You heard Pastor Sloan speak a few weeks ago. The anti-Christ could be a baby or a grown-up, actually walking the streets of Europe. These are the end times. I heard the voice. I had to obey the divine command."

"That was not God's voice Gary. Either it was auto-suggestion or worse, the voice of a demon. Satan somehow disguises himself as an angel of light to delude us. God's voice never urges us to sin. A man came to me telling me that the Lord had told him who he was to marry. I asked him if he had approached the lady. "Not yet," he said. He was waiting for her husband to die. Of course, this was nonsense Gary," the pastor smiled.

"My mission was to kill the anti-Christ. I had to obey God not man."

The pastor sighed deeply. It was obvious that this poor soul was totally convinced of his divine appointment. He was dangerously obsessed and deluded. He remembered counselling a man who believed that the graffiti on the walls were messages from the UVF to kill him. He also believed they used headlines in the national newspapers. Irrational obsessions, like rats gnawing at this soul. Gary was an extreme case. "Let me pray with you, Gary, before I go."

"I just got in in the nick of time. Another half minute and the baby would have been dead. The little bastard had been hanging around like a bad smell for a few weeks. Apologetically hovering like he always did. He was quieter than usual. He had suggested on a number of occasions that if Gina and I were to go out, he would be more than willing to babysit. We never dreamed what was on his mind."

"It makes you think, people could be sitting opposite you, smiling at you, and all the while planning to murder you," mused Les, a big broad second row forward.

"You're reading my mind mate. It's your turn," quipped Adrian, a small, dark, athletic looking chap with black wiry hair.

The three were seated at a table in a local rugby club in the east Belfast area, on the second floor of a modern pavilion surrounded on three sides by cricket and rugby pitches. Extensive windows gave a panoramic view of green grass and distant trees.

"What's your poison boys?" asked Les.

"A pint of Guinness for me," smiled Tim.

"And a pint of Guinness for me," echoed Adrian.

Les went up to the long traditional bar and came back to the table, three pints wrapped in his huge hands.

"Thanks Herman Munster," chirped Adrian.

"Remember yer a wee man, short arse," retorted Les.

"Aye, but dynamite comes in small packages."

"So does poison. Now shut up. Go on with your story Tim."

"Well, one night Gina was going shopping with her mother. Her mother picked her up and dropped off Gary. 'I'll pick Gary up on the way back. He so wanted to come and see the baby.' This was strange because I got the impression he resented the baby as much as he resented me. It was as if we had stolen his sister you know. Anyway, I made some tea and a sandwich. We watched TV, yes, I remember 'Mastermind' was on. He's a bright spark. He answered most of the general knowledge questions. It was time for me to put the wee one to bed. He was hungry. His nappy was soaking, so I decided to give him a bath. I ran the water, put in the Johnson's Baby Bath. It was all suds and bubbles. Well, my guts had been playin' me up all day, and I was suffering from a dose of the runs."

"You mean you were inadvertently discharging effluent," interjected Adrian in a very posh voice.

"Aye, you're 'effluent' in three languages wee man. Give over," scolded Les.

Tim continued. "I summoned Gary and asked him to look after the baby while I answered the emergency call. No sooner had I sat down when I heard a terrible commotion. The baby began to cry and I could hear Gary shouting hysterically 'Die anti-Christ, die! Die anti-Christ, die!'"

"That's creepy," commented Les.

"My God!" added Adrian.

"Anyway, I got out of the toilet cubicle next to the bathroom, and tried to open the door. The little git had locked it, and I was standing there 'Open the door Gary! Open the door! Let me in! Let me in!' to no avail. Then I kicked the bloody thing in, you wouldn't believe it."

"All right fellas, I'll see you next week at practice," interrupted a team mate as he made his way out of the bar.

"OK Jonesy." They waved in unison.

"Go on," urged Adrian.

"It's still surreal. Gary was in the bath. He was standing on my baby, trying to drown him. I'll never forget the wild insane look in his eyes, and all the while screaming 'Die anti-Christ, die! Die anti-Christ, die!'"

"What did you do then," asked Les impatiently.

"I pulled Gary out of the bath and out the door. I rescued the child from beneath the water. The bastard bolted down the stairs and out of the house. The wee one recovered quickly after I applied mouth to mouth resuscitation to him. I wrapped him in a blanket, put him in his car seat and took him to Dundonald Hospital. I 'phoned the police and Gina from there on my mobile."

"That boy was a bottle short of a six pack, eh?" said Adrian shaking his head in disbelief.

"Had I been a few moments later, my son would be dead."

"Is this guy some kind of religious nutter? Ye know, working miracles and casting demons out of door knobs?" asked Les.

"Aye, like one o' those Yankee Prosperity Poopers, more interested in profits than prophets," added Adrian.

"The pastor of the church is a decent, well-balanced man, but some of the visiting speakers are off the wall. They had a prophetic conference a few months ago, you know 'the end is nigh' and all that."

"Aye, the end is nigh as far as my drink's concerned. I'll have another Guinness please Adrian."

The congregation, primed by prayer and praise, hung on Pastor Sloan's every word.

"Only the spotless Lamb of God is worthy to open the Seven Seals on the heavenly scroll to unleash the judgement of God on this world. The Four Horsemen of the Apocalypse gallop out. The White Horse, ridden by the Anti-Christ signifies success by propaganda and political guile. The Red Horse brandishes a red sword dripping with the blood of carnage and war."

Three elderly ladies, thoroughly enjoying the display before them, pass around a bag of sweets; but the noisy crackle of the paper as they opened it, is drowned by the preacher's voice.

"The Black Horse speaks of famine and the Pale Horse heralds death in all its forms. Meteor showers bombard the earth. This is the great day of God's wrath"

A young, embarrassed, mother moves apologetically out of the pew as she comforts her wailing infant; startling an aged bespectacled gentleman who has gently nodded off at the end of the row.

"Then follows the Judgement of the Seven Vials, or Bowls, of God's wrath. Evil sores break out on the followers of The Beast. All the water on the earth will turn to blood. The sun becomes hotter. The Euphrates River is dried up, making way for the hordes of the east as they career madly to

Armageddon, and unimaginable slaughter. A massive earthquake ruins the great cities of the world. Washington, Moscow, Rome and all the pomp, power and pride of man will crumble before his eyes."

An old lady is helped from her seat to a rollator by an elder, who assists her to the back of the hall.

"But that is not all," boomed the impassioned preacher, "Seven Angels shall blow seven trumpets of further judgement. Fiery hail burns a third of the earth. The solar system is knocked out of kilter. Horrible demonic beings, Locusts of the Abyss, are loosed by the Angel of the Bottomless Pit. They torment, but do not kill, humanity."

A mother lightly smacks her miscreant son across the back of the head. He has just flicked the ear of a young girl his own age in the pew in front.

"But take heart beloved. Our Lord will come again and set up His Eternal Kingdom. He shall reign for ever and ever!"

Loud 'Amens' from the congregation. 'Hallelujah! Maranatha! Lord come quickly! Praise to Him who sits upon the Throne of the Universe!'

A surging crescendo of praise filled the hall with adoration.

After he fled from the house and ran from the tree-lined middle-class suburbs where his sister and her family lived, he was at a loss where to go. He walked a few miles down the main road to the hall where his family worshipped. He was shaking. He could feel the sweat trickle down the small of his back. He was dressed in only jeans and shirt. He was feverish even though the evening was chilly. Darkness had fallen. The shop fronts glared brightly. Golden leaves had begun to litter the pavement.

He made his way through a maze of streets that lay in the shadow of the two great cranes that stood sentinel at the head of the lough. Painted bright yellow, with the black Harland and Wolff logo on them, they dominated the Belfast skyline.

He found himself, as in a dream, outside the hall. The mid-week prayer meeting had just finished, and the last attendees were trickling out, sent on their way by a church elder he recognised and respected. He walked to the door, "Hello Mr Galbraith. Is the pastor about?"

"Well Gary. How are you son? You look a bit under the weather. The pastor's not here tonight, I led the meeting instead. Can I help you?"

"Could I please talk to you. It's very important."

Elder Galbraith guided Gary into a small, plain, but tastefully decorated, room with white walls, blue carpet and a large desk. It had shelves on the walls and had an air of study and meditation about it.

"The pastor won't mind us using his office for a while," smiled the older man. He was dressed in a fading sports jacket with leather patches on the elbows, dark trousers and black shoes. His hands were large, gnarled and weather-beaten; the hands of a retired bricklayer.

"Well son?" How can I help you?" he queried.

Gary was distraught and confused. His hands wrestled with each other on his lap. "Can the anti-Christ be stopped?"

"Boy! That's a question and a half."

"Can he?" urged Gary.

"The prophets of the Old Testament made hundreds of prophecies concerning The Lord Jesus. We cannot change what God has ordained. Remember Herod tried to get him, slaughtered all the babies in the Bethlehem area after the Wise Men dodged him. The Messiah had to be born to redeem us. Nothing could stop it. Nothing can stop his return, and nothing can stop the events leading up to his return, and that includes the reign of the anti-Christ."

"So you're saying the Anti-Christ can't be stopped!" shouted Gary. "Surely, he can be stopped. The Lord could not give orders to kill him unless he could be stopped. You have to be wrong Mr Galbraith; you have to be wrong."

"Easy son, easy."

Gary burst into tears. He wept convulsively. Mr Galbraith pulled out a handkerchief, put his big hand on Gary's shoulder, and tried hard to comfort the boy.

The door thumped loudly, and three uniformed policemen burst into the room.

In retrospect, Gary was appalled and disgusted at what he had done. The judge ruled that he should be psychiatrically assessed. The report stated that Gary should not stand trial due to the imbalance of his mind. He was incarcerated in a mental institution in Scotland, until the psychiatric experts deemed he was not a danger to the public. After three years he was released, and was welcomed back into the loving arms of his parents and the Zion Covenant Tabernacle. He worked voluntarily in various charity organisations until he entered university to pursue a degree. His parents, friends and pastor advised history rather than theology.

His brother-in-law, Tim, never forgave Gary, and forbade him to cross the threshold of his home ever again.

His forgiving sister Gina, brought the child to her parents' house now and then. Under her close supervision, Gary was allowed to form a distant but friendly relationship with the boy. An apparently bright and gifted four-year-old.

The Twilight Department

What a wonderful day I've had," laughed Ronnie joyfully as he tossed his folded newspaper casually on the table. "The bus run was great. We boarded outside the church. Marvellous. There must have been thirty of us."

"Quicksilver Tours," quipped Ronnie's son Johnny. "Walking stick Warriors. The onset of the living dead!"

"We may be in God's waiting room but there's plenty of life in us yet!", grinned Ronnie, gently cuffing Johnny as he passed by on the way to the kitchen. "Pizzaro was fifty-four when he conquered Peru, Moses was eighty when he was called into Egypt. I'm immortal until I'm called home."

"Come on old man," Johnny took a fighter's pose, and the two cuffed each other lightly.

The doorbell ding-donged and Ronnie, breaking off the skirmish, went out of the living room and into the hall to answer.

"Saved by the bell Rip Van Winkle!" jeered Johnny.

"Watch it, watch it Johnny boy!" Ronnie threatened.

The sun was receding in the west and its fading rays flooded through the trembling leaves of a tree, one of many that lined the wide avenue where they lived. He opened the door to two official looking people, a man and a woman, each wearing a name tag.

She was a middle-aged lady, of slight build, short hair in a dark coat and tightly worn skirt. She personified efficiency and order. "Prunella Potts" Ronnie thought.

He was a rather awkward little man, and looked uncomfortable in his grey suit and dark tie. His head, larger than average, was bald with a greying fringe around the back. "Chrome dome," thought Ronnie.

He was first to speak after coughing nervously. "Hello, we're from the Ministry of Health, Twilight Department. I am Maurice Beasley, and this is Miss Wilmer." At this they both indicated the name tags affixed to the lapels on their respective jackets.

"What can I do for you?" asked Ronnie.

"Ahh, it's rather a delicate matter. May we come in?" smiled Beasley.

"Well, it's a bit inconvenient at present."

"This is extremely important," interrupted Miss Wilmer in a clipped imperative tone.

"OK," relented Ronnie, and showed them both into the snug tidy parlour where he entertained guests. The parlour looked onto the avenue, now covered in the golden glow of autumn leaves as the world turned and seasons changed.

"Have a seat," Ronnie indicated a sofa that occupied the bay window which glowed warmly in the golden rays of the departing sunlight which dappled the walls with gently moving leafy patterns.

"Just to make sure we have our man, as it were," Beasley smiled smugly at his little joke revealing a row of yellowish, uneven teeth. "I shall now defer to Miss Wilmer."

"Himmler," thought Ronnie. She was just like him; nondescript, receding chin; gold round rimmed glasses that gave her grey eyes a persistent, brooding gimlet stare. She reached into a slim leather briefcase and extracted a thin brown file. She opened it and began.

"You are Mr Ronald Arthur Glover of 1A Ashworth Avenue, Belfast BT5 6GO."

"Yes."

"You were born just over eighty years ago."

Ronnie nodded.

"Your insurance number is BT 07 75 X."

"Yes."

"That seems to be in order Mr Beasley," she concluded in her formal clipped tone. "This indeed is our client."

"I'm sure you've heard of our department Mr, er, Glover. We operate within the Health Services. We were set up some years ago due to public demand."

"Government cuts more like," interjected Ronnie. "They've been stripping the Health Service of resources for years. Just to encourage privatisation. Profit before people. Pennywise, pound foolish. They deliberately create poverty, yet poverty costs a country more in resources. It's just stupid."

"Really we're not here to discuss politics," snapped Miss Wilmer icily. "Our job is to implement policy and apply the will of Parliament."

Ronnie looked at her; a typical bureaucrat; a stickler for the rules; obedient to the rules, no matter where they led. No need to think, or exercise discretion or be guided by morality or compassion. The rules to her were everything. Her thin lips were pressed over her small perfect teeth, surmounted by a pinched and pointed nose. The light glinted on her spectacles, giving her a sinister spectral quality. There would be no mercy from this woman.

"Let's get down to business," Beasley smiled. "As I'm sure you are aware Mr Glover, our department presides over the smooth departure of our more senior citizens. We have been in existence for ten years now and so far, on the whole, our processes, stemming from the law, have worked rather well." He took off his glasses, pulled out a white handkerchief from the side pocket of his jacket, and began to polish the lenses. "It has come to our attention, Mr Glover, that you are about to reach the fulfilment of the time the government has allotted before the next stage, as it were." He gave a little nervous chuckle.

"But I thought that was voluntary," protested Ronnie. "I'm not ready to go yet. I've a full enjoyable life. I can look after myself. I don't need a carer, I've family who care."

"Well, it used to be optional, but because of, shall we say, political, social and of course moral forces, the government made it compulsory for those who had reached a certain age."

"Financial force to save money you mean. What's moral about putting people to death. Who gives them the right to decide in place of the Almighty? Tell your bosses I'm not interested!"

"You've no need to be so aggressive," snapped Miss Wilmer. "We're only doing our job."

"Agh! The camp guards at Auschwitz were only doing their jobs. The soldiers who carried out mass murder in eastern Europe were only doing their job. The murderers who beheaded their prisoners in the Middle East and put it on a video were only doing their job!" Ronnie was becoming angrier and his voice rose with every sentence. "I'm not ready to go and no bloody fascist in no bloody government is going to make me!"

"There really is no need to be offensive Mr Glover. As Miss Wilmer says, we're merely public servants."

"Thugs! Serving the public by bumping them off."

The door opened suddenly and Johnny burst into the room. "What's going on here? Are you alright dad? Are these people upsetting you?"

"They're here to tell me I'm ready for the next stage!" smiled Ronnie.

"What do ye mean?" asked a puzzled Johnny.

"The next stage son. They're going to launch me into eternity, compliments of our so-called benign democratic government."

"We don't make the rules Mr Glover. You really are over dramatising this whole business."

"You're telling me the government is going to legally put me to death. So sorry for being dramatic!"

"Right!" interjected Johnny. "I've heard of you creeps, Government Ghouls, pushing the elderly over the brink of eternity. Get the hell out of here while you still can!"

Terror galvanised the pair, who rose hurriedly from their seats, Beasley with some difficulty.

"Look at ya," commented Johnny. "My da's fitter than you are! What are you going to do when they come for you, ye ol' bastard ye! Get out the pair of you!"

"Don't you touch me, I'll 'phone the police," squealed Miss Wilmer.

"Don't worry about being touched love. You haven't been touched by a man in decades. You make Medusa look like Snow White. Now piss off the pair of ye and don't come back!"

Johnny virtually hunted the two civil servants from the parlour into the hall, and into the gloaming of the autumn evening.

A week passed. Ronnie had just prepared dinner for Johnny who was seated at the table in the kitchen cum dining room. It faced onto the small back garden. Wheelie bins were backed up outside the large window.

"Well dad, how is Mr Methuselah today?"

"No cheek sonny boy! I control the foodstuffs, and you might get them over your head instead of on yer plate," joked Ronnie.

"Harken to the Deadly Dreadnought. Where do you bury your dead dad?"

"On the subject of dying," grinned Ronnie as he ladled Irish stew onto Johnny's plate before returning it to the stove. "I had this letter from the Department of Health. Anyway, I'll read it to you. 'Dear Mr Glover etc etc.... You received a visit from two of our operators on the blah, blah, blah who informed you of your imminent departure. They have made a formal complaint to us, that they were insulted, verbally abused, before being physically ejected from your home.''

"Bloody right too," interrupted Johnny.

"'We are reluctant to use coercion in this matter, but unless we have your complete compliance, we shall have no alternative but to call upon the Police Service to enforce the rule of law.'"

"They're going to get the cops to make sure you turn up for your own hanging. The charge – you are eighty years old. This is totally out of order dad. This is just not on! It's incredible. It would be funny if it wasn't so tragic." Johnny put down his spoon. "Is there no-body you can see dad? I mean, a local councillor, or M.P.?"

"I've already tried son. They told me, 'This is the law of the land.' It's been passed through Parliament and there is nothing they can do. They appear to be sympathetic, but they say they are helpless."

"Helpless my ass! This is barbarism at its worst! It's back to the Stone Age where the old and weak were thrown out of the tribe and exposed to the elements to die. Who would have believed it?" complained Johnny.

"Who would have believed that there are supposed to be one hundred and fifty different genders and counting? Who would have believed that men would marry men? Who could have foreseen that millions of babies would be murdered in their mothers' wombs? Someone can be done for kicking a cat, yet it's considered quite normal to kill an unborn child," commented Ronnie sadly.

"Aye, and all in the name of love and concern. We love the old so much so let's bump them off just in case they suffer. There, that poor girl will ruin her education if she goes through with her pregnancy. Humans slaughtered at both ends of the human scale in the name of love, by liberal democracies, cut loose from any form of morality but their own. It's sick dad. It's so sick. It's not goin' to happen to you dad. It's just not," vowed Johnny.

"Away back in the twenty twenties they brought in an Assisted Suicide Bill. Some public representatives hit out at the growing obsession with death as a solution. They protested that it threatened to undermine the fundamental morality at the core of our nation. There was this guy in Switzerland who invented 'suicide-pods'. They were like coffins. You could climb in, close the airtight lid and press a button to quickly reduce the oxygen inside. You were born after the great worldwide Covid 19 Pandemic."

"I've heard of it, but thank God, I never experienced it."

"Well, many people ended up in hospital. There was a great furore over the fact that children with mental and physical handicaps had a DNR note attached to their charts."

"DNR?" queried Johnny.

"Do Not Resuscitate. It came on the back of a court ruling that people with Down's Syndrome and foetal abnormalities could be aborted in the womb. There was a kick up at the time, and the hospitals apologised. At least some people in society cared at that time. But that's ancient history. Ten years in, abortion, in many cases, became compulsory. So much for the Healthcare Bill."

"How can they care for you and keep you healthy if you're dead?" Johnny shook his head.

"They take care of you alright, like the gangsters in prohibition Chicago used to do in the nineteen thirties."

"You dirty rat. Don't speak to me direct. OK. I'm the boss. Speak to Vinnie and he speaks to me. Alright! Dog face!" bantered Johnny.

"Go on you big eejit," laughed Ronnie, and threw the pen he was holding at him.

"You'll get a wooden overcoat and a pair of concrete boots gramps. Watch it," teased Johnny in an exaggerated transatlantic accent.

"Get out Spats Lonegan!"

"Well love, how are ye getting on? Are all the kids well?"

"Aye da, we're managing. Five of them now, all steps and stairs. If anything, Peter and I are fertile. He says he's afraid to look at me or I'll get pregnant."

A little plump dark-haired toddler waddled unsteadily towards Ronnie, his arms outstretched. "Ganda!" he called. Ronnie put him on his knees and played 'Horses' with him. Infant chuckles filled the room. Baby's eyes were filled with happiness and glee.

"And we're off for the great Granda/Child race. Jockey Noel Gordon has got off to a great start on the much fancied 'Old Contemptible'. They approach the first fence and up they come and Old Contemptible leaps like a deer over." Ronnie grabs the child in two hands and throws his knees up. "And Noel Gordon is over. He takes the lead over two, three, four fences. He's coming into the lead, and Noel Gordon on Old Contemptible wins by a short head.

"Gain Ganda!" shouted Noel, milk teeth showing in his pudgy face.

"Leave Granda alone Noel. He's breathing like a grampus."

She gradually extricated him from his grandfather's knees and held him in her arms.

"He'll have you at that all day!"

"Sure, he's no harm. What's it like living down the road, love?"

"Alright. It's a bit rough and the house is small but we're making do. Ye get a bit of fighting and drunkenness at weekends but it's tolerable."

"I was thinking love. Maybe if I cashed my chips in you could have my house."

"What do you mean?"

"Well two people from the government were out to see me over a week ago about popping my clogs. Ye know. Passing over."

"Passing over where?"

"God girl you're slow on the uptake. They told me my allotted time was up and I'd have to move on. They were there to make arrangements but Johnny ran them out o' the house."

"Dad, we love you. Don't feel under pressure to depart this life because our finances are not the best. They'll get better. We only have you once dad. You are precious to all of us. Even Peter believes you're one true gentleman; though the jury's out on Johnny."

"Are you sure love?"

"Dad" she set the baby in a little pram, knelt down beside her father and hugged him. "Don't you fret yourself about us. We'll be fine. We want you around for as long as we can possibly have you. The kids love you," she comforted.

"A few years ago, a good friend of mine took really ill. Her children surrounded her bed in a side ward in the hospital. It was 'mammy this' and 'mammy that'; 'mammy we love you and don't want to see you suffering'; 'it might be better if you passed on'; 'we need the house, we need the money, we're up to our ears in debt'. Lydia, I know she didn't want to die. Her government time wasn't even up, but the pressure they put on her was terrible, underhand, surreptitious and subtle. I visited her before the end. I can still hear her sobbing into her pillows. She acquiesced to the Assisted Suicide Scheme. She was down, forsaken and rejected. It would have brought tears to a stone," recalled Ronnie.

There was a commotion at the front door as the other four children, 'the troops' invaded. They made a beeline for Ronnie with cries of "It's Granda – get him!" and flung themselves upon him with ferocious zeal, to the amusement of Lydia and Peter who had to rush to rescue him from the chaotic scrum. The infant Noel cried delightedly from his pram "Gain Ganda gain!"

"What did you call them, Chrome Dome and Mrs Himmler are at the door, and there's two peelers with them. They're in for a surprise," Johnny was looking out of a small narrow window at the side of the front door. He took out his mobile 'phone and made two quick 'phone calls. Then, with his father behind him he opened the door.

It was two weeks since their last visit. The autumn evening was blustery and the dry leaves rustled in the avenue beyond the gardens. The clouds, ominous and threatening, were rimmed dark red as the sun departed and the world turned.

"We're here to see Mr Glover, your father I believe," began Mr Beasley, his large head reflecting the light of a street lamp.

"A light to light the Gentiles," thought Johnny.

"I'm here," said Ronnie, stepping forward.

"We're here to transport you to our headquarters Mr Glover. Could you please be reasonable? We really do not wish to call upon the officers here. We sent you a letter by registered post a number of days ago."

"I received it, but I refuse to comply in what is tantamount to my own murder."

"No dramas please," spat Miss Wilmer, looking like a bespectacled wraith in the darkening light, "We're here to enforce the law."

A car screeched to a halt. Out tumbled Peter, Lydia holding Noel, and 'the troops'. They pushed up the garden path, jostled the police and the two civil servants unceremoniously out of the way, and entered the hallway.

"You're not going to take my da away," Lydia addressed the police. "Two of you not enough, eh? They've got a minibus full of cops in riot gear round the corner."

"It's a bloody fascist state," shouted Johnny.

The avenue became crowded. Two minibuses pulled up outside. A group of about sixteen fit young men poured out of one.

"There's my local football team. Dead on time. This way boys!" shouted Johnny.

They poured into the front garden and surrounded the huddled official delegation at the front door.

"Welcome lads," waved Johnny, and another contingent of young men jumped from the other minibus and thronged into the now packed garden. Three fluters and a drummer struck up 'Men of Harlech', 'We'll Fight but not Surrender' and 'Dolly's Brae'.

To add to the growing melee, members of the Anti-Euthanasia Society of Northern Ireland, turned up in a number of cars and were joined by ministers from the mainline churches in the area, in a rare display of ecumenical harmony and solidarity. Although the small police riot squad did dismount from their vehicle, the officer in charge, exercising discretion and common sense, ordered them back in again.

Mr Beasley, his head reflecting light in the gloom, was jostled to and fro. Miss Wilmer's squeals could be heard punctuating the strident tunes of 'Abide with Me' and 'We are the Billy Boys'.

The delegation, well and truly routed, was hissed and booed with cries of "Should be ashamed of yourselves!" and "You're not going to kill my granda!" and "Away back to the concentration camp! Bloody Gestapo!"

The two policemen incurred minor cuts and bruises. They lost their hats which were ceremoniously burned by the rougher elements of the band as a portent of better days to come. They were heard to grumble "Wee gits", with reference to the older children who had waded into them and kicked them on the shins.

After the people were praised and thanked by Johnny and his dad; when the different factions had congratulated each other; when the tunes and the strident drumbeat ceased; the crowd melted away into the autumn darkness. The startled neighbours closed their doors and turned out their lights and the family were left to discuss the future over a cup of tea.

"What about going to Russia, Ronnie?" suggested his son-in-law, Peter. "There's no compulsory euthanasia there."

"Ironic, isn't it? The old Soviet Union, the old atheistic Empire of Satan is now the Russian Federation and, under the influence of the Russian Orthodox Church, has banned euthanasia, voluntary or otherwise. Now we, the one-time upholders of Christian values, have destroyed these values by killing our unborn and aged on an industrial scale. All in the name of love for mankind." Ronnie shook his head. "Who would have believed it? Anyway, my passport's been cancelled. I'd have to be smuggled out of the country."

Johnny smiled. "I can see the wanted poster now da, the hue and cry for the Geriatric Jesse James. This man is dangerous. His wrinkles are contagious!" The others couldn't help laughing.

Peter joked, "In the early days there were groups of pensioners who headed for the hills to evade the law. They lived rough in the forests and the mountains."

"For how long Pete. Sure at our age we couldn't stick that life for long. It would be a bit like the poor native Americans driven off their lands to be put on a reservation. Most of them had to reluctantly drift back and accept what the government doled out to them on the reservation."

"Yeah dad. But even that government didn't put the poor souls to death," protested Lydia.

"We'll just have to change public opinion folks. It was wonderful to see all these people turn out tonight. There is opposition to this bloody sacrilege," Peter clenched his teeth. "The scary thing though is that this has been going on for at least ten years. The protest tonight was a voice in the wilderness of the corporate liberal west," argued Pete, his dark eyes full of sadness. "They legislate according to the values of parliament and society. They camouflage the profit motive and operate under the blanket of pretended concern and love. How disgusting," added Peter. "The light that is in them is darkness."

Everyone was disturbed by a fracas in the other room. The children, initially excited and delighted by their contribution to the previous disturbance, were extremely tired.

"We need to go Daddy," Lydia stood up. Ronnie stood up and they embraced. Father and daughter.

"All the best Ronnie," Peter held out his hand.

After rounding up 'the troops', they took their leave. Little Noel, carried in his mother's arms, and surprisingly still awake, shouted "Gain Ganda! Gain Ganda!"

"Well son," Ronnie noted, "after all the shenanigans of tonight, I know I'm loved."

"Don't worry dad. I love ya, well most of the time anyway. Give me yer money!"

"Ye cheeky git!"

Three days later Ronnie enjoyed himself immensely as he socialised with old friends on a bus run through the Antrim Glens and along the Coast Road. For creation, it was show time, in a still warm and glorious autumn day. He drank in the panorama of sea and sky, scudding clouds, sun shimmering sea. The deep green beauty of the valleys with their farmsteads, livestock and clashing rivers.

All seemed clear to him. His vision and consciousness were heightened. He was one with it all, yet a distinct personality, plurality in unity. It was a symphony of colour and birdsong stretching as far as his old eyes could see, and beyond. He was in tune with the pulse, throb and rhythm of the universe and its creator.

After a wonderful lunch at a restaurant, he wandered off to a bench that overlooked the water. He could make out Rathlin to the north west, and some of the Scottish islands lazing in the haze straight ahead. His reverie scanned his eventful life, childhood, youth, manhood. His first kiss and fight and job; his marriage, children, widowerhood. He saw it all before him, like a distant world, a planet no less.

He felt a heavy hand on his shoulder, and heard the gruff policeman's voice, "Mr Glover?"

"Yes," he turned. Two uniformed police stood with Mr Beasley and Miss Wilmer. The diabolic duo. Chrome Dome and Himmler. A marriage made in a filing cabinet and measured out in paper clips.

The family never saw Ronnie again. He was taken to a rambling house somewhere in the Castlereagh hills, the once home of a linen baron, now part of Health and Social Services. The autumn sun set as the unmarked police car drove Ronnie through the gates which automatically closed after him.

Johnny, Lydia and Peter, along with some of the more unruly elements of the band, were charged with various assaults on the two civil servants and the police. All received suspended sentences.

"Better not to make martyrs of them," commented Miss Wilmer imperiously.

"Oh yes indeed," agreed Mr Maurice Beasley, taking off his glasses and rubbing them vigorously with his handkerchief. "Oh yes indeed."

As the family came out of court, there were no cameras, no reporters, in fact, no media coverage at all.

Three days after his disappearance, a package arrived at his home by registered post. A reinforced cardboard box containing a tubular metal box. An official letter stated "The final remains and ashes of Mr Ronald Glover. Courtesy of the Twilight Department, DHSS.

CHAPTER FIVE

The Great Ballysillan Post Office Robbery

"Ballysillan Post Office! That's it! It'll solve all our problems Tubby!" Jake rubbed his hands fastidiously, eyes smiling in his lazy aquiline face. "Roll us a feg will ya mate, I'm gaspin'. I'm all out of tobacco."

"Do ya think my name's Bill Gates or something. This has got to do me to my next dole day!" grumbled Tubby, a fat roly-poly guy who lived up to his name. "What are ye rambling on about Ballysillan Post office for?"

They sat in the kitchen of a house situated in a large housing estate in the west of the city. The window looked onto a small back garden with a patch of unkempt grass, a shed and a large plastic wheelie bin.

It was raining and water poured from a broken spout onto the concrete beneath the eaves. A brown wooden fence with a wide battered gate cordoned the garden off from a communal back alley.

"How much did you say we owed big Sammy?" asked Jake, his long frame leaning against the sink, taking the proffered roll-up.

"Three hundred pounds, and we'll be lookin' for a new set o' knee caps if he doesn't get his money on time. I told you not to go near him. He makes Genghis Khan look like Basil Brush." Tubby blinked his eyes empathetically (especially when he was under pressure). He sat at a simple table, the remnants of a fry on his plate, rolling a cigarette of his own.

Jake stood up to his normal lofty height – he resembled a pull through for a rifle or a human toilet brush. "We rob the Post Office. We hit it on a Thursday when people cash their dole cheque or pension money. It'll be easy."

"What! Away and feel yer head Jake, as if we haven't got enough trouble. We're not long out o' jail, and you said 'Oh it'll be easy'. Oh yeah – an easy six months in the clink."

"We need to pay off that big git McCabe don't we?" urged Jake.

"We've nearly got that money saved up." He sees Jake's head look down towards the tiled floor. "Haven't we?" He blinked in desperation as dread made his stomach flip over.

"I meant to tell you about that mate. I lost it."

"What do you mean you lost it! How?" Tubby rose up from the chair and became animated.

Jake took a drag of the roll-up and blew the smoke towards the ceiling. He was restless and uncomfortable.

"How did you lose it?" continued Tubby between clenched teeth, eyes that were two Belisha Beacons glaring at Jake.

"I was drunk, got into a card school. I'm sorry mate."

"Don't sorry me. You're always bloody sorry mate. Your head's so far up your arse you could give yourself your own MRI scan!"

"It's done mate, I'm sorry. I can't change it," pleaded Jake apologetically.

"McCabe will be changing our faces. We'll be looking like the lost brothers of the Hunchback of Notre Dame!" He makes a contorted grimace. "We'll be hearing bells alright when that scumbag and his hombres start on us with baseball bats."

"That's why we need to do the Post Office Tubby!"

"What do you mean 'we'! 'We' never lost the money on a card game! YOU did! So, YOU do it. Leave me out of it!"

"But Tubby, we need to pay yer man off," pleaded Jake. "We're mincemeat if we don't! He's expecting pay off from both of us."

"Oh, you're a real true friend you are. Partners together eh," sneered Tubby.

"Yeah, Harland and Wolff, Marks and Spencer, Holmes and Watson."

"More like Morecambe and Wise. Ya scumbag."

They had grown up together in the rough streets of working-class Belfast. Both from dysfunctional families, both dragged up by, sometimes two, but mostly one parent. Both entered the judicial system at twelve years old, after a long litany of petty crime, theft and burglaries.

Then came the young offenders centre, the penalty for constant criminality, as, like so many others, they spun through the revolving door of recidivism.

"Come on mate. I need your help. Remember you were released from the Young Offenders Centre and your family had moved? Who took you in, me and my ma."

"They never even told me they were moving. So much for happy families," groaned Tubby.

"It must have been your lovely blue eyes," quipped Jake.

"They'll be black if we don't give yer man his money. We'll be like two Giant Pandas," moaned Tubby.

"You're in then. You're a good lad Tubby. This is how we go about it."

As they descended the hill down Ballysillan Road, they could see the giants Samson and Goliath straddling what was once the largest dry dock in the world; iconic symbols of a shipyard that led the world in technology and skill. The Olympic, Canberra, The Britannia, and of course the queen of them all, the ill-fated Titanic; the supreme example of man's pride and arrogance, judged by the iceberg in the cold Atlantic.

"Is that gun safe?" asked Tubby nervously.

"Don't worry. No bullets in it. We'll have to give Squealer fifty quid after the job. He borrowed it from a certain organisation."

The sun was shining on the two great yellow cranes. To the right, nestling in the fold of the Holywood hills, was the great ornate white house of Stormont, seat of the government of Northern Ireland, radiant in the Spring sunshine.

In those days Ballysillan Post Office doubled as a grocery store and 'minimart'. As they entered from the main road into the shop, they were confronted with a long counter. At one end, near the door, was the Post office section where a number of Old Age Pensioners, queued to lift their weekly pensions. There were two small openings in a protective Perspex glass screen that stretched half way down the counter. One half of the shop was given over to the butcher's and cold meats counter; while the other was divided into aisles for bread, biscuits etc.

The two robbers, by this time sporting balaclavas that they donned just before entering, passed by the queue around between the aisles, and approached the Post Office section via the butchery counter.

"Hands up! Hands up!" yelled Jake excitedly, brandishing an old revolver, clearly a relic from the Second World War. He was obviously hyper nervous.

"Keep calm and nobody gets hurt," shouted Tubby.

Jake, animated by a mixture of over enthusiasm, fear and an adrenalin rush, knocked the heavy white marble bacon slicer off the counter and onto his foot with a dull "Crunch!".

"Agh!" He screamed and started to jump up and down, attempting to hold the injured foot with one hand while still trying to look like a menacing armed robber.

"What the hell are ye doing," shouted Tubby, shocked at the unexpected turn of events. This was definitely not in the plan concocted by these two criminal masterminds.

A fierce looking old lady, formerly a resident of the Shankill Road, realised quickly what was going on and determined that no-one was going to steal her pension that she had 'worked her fingers to the bone' to obtain.

Like a pit bull terrier who believes it is about to be deprived of its bone, false teeth gnashing, she launched herself at the two hapless miscreants, one still jumping up and down, the other petrified by fear.

With ferocious gusto she set upon the enemy with her hand bag, swinging and slashing like Henry V at Agincourt.

There could be only one winner. The poor bandits were routed. With determined blows and the war cry "Cheeky bastards" on her lips, she beat the would-be gangsters from the premises as would a gladiator from a Roman amphitheatre.

The victims ran out onto the road outside the shop, only to be run down by a car that braked just in time not to kill them, but throw them over the bonnet.

The customers who gathered at the door watched wide-eyed as the two bandits hobbled up Ballysillan Road, Jake's hand on Tubby's shoulder as they made for the potential safety of the concrete maze of the estate.

When calm and order were restored, the faint hearted comforted, the 'pit bull terrier' praised as the intrepid heroine of the moment, the police arrived. They took statements and viewed the CCTV both inside and outside the Post Office.

Of course, Jake and Tubby were known only too well to them, and were soon picked up the next day. By this time, Jake had a plaster cast on the injured foot. The police also acquired the gun used in the robbery. There were no bullets in it which meant a lighter sentence.

When arraigned in court, they made no application for bail, considering it would be safer on the inside than being prey to the psychopathic propensities of Sammy McCabe. This was a wise move. The man they had promised to pay to provide the gun, was found knee-capped down a back alley for losing what he had secretly borrowed and had failed to return.

After a time on remand, Jake and Tubby were sentenced. They duly settled down to do their 'bird'. Prison was almost like home and they attained a certain amount of, shall we say, notoriety, in both police and criminal worlds as well as locally. They became legendary as the two eejits who attempted to carry out 'The Great Ballysillan Post Office Robbery'.

CHAPTER SIX

The Jawbone of an Ox

"**G**ive me the strength of Samson!" he screamed, his face red with the blood-rush and contorted with rage. He had just burst into our kitchen from the street, and adopted a karate stance in the middle of the floor. "AAGGGH!" he yelled panting, as he stood before us. My mother's eyes were wide with shock, like incredulous saucers, as she recognised the normally quiet and polite young Christian man who, until his marriage, had been a frequent visitor to her house.

"What's the matter?" I asked, jumping up from my chair.

"I want to smite the Philistines," he yelled, "They just threw me out of the Smoothing Iron." This was the nickname of a pub that resembled the base of a flat iron, at the top of Templemore Avenue and the junction of the Beersbridge Road. The 'Blue Bar' was the proper name, a tough dive, the haunt of hard men and paramilitaries.

"It took six of them to get me out. They barred the door behind me. They wouldn't come out."

He was about thirty-five, a short and stocky guy, supple and athletic, short blonde hair and very clear blue eyes. He was also very skilled in the noble lethal art of karate.

He kicked up and out, and his foot whizzed past my ear. Even in drink he was controlled. Had he been serious, I would have been unconscious. A salvo of straight arm punches was delivered to the air at lightning speed. I flung my arms around him and held him fast until he calmed down.

"Easy mate, easy, settle down."

"I want to kill somebody. I don't want to settle down. I am so bloody tired of all the crap. I have had enough of turning the other cheek. I want to kill the bastards."

"OK, OK, ease off. Sit down and we'll talk about it."

"Talk, talk, talk. That's all God does but there's no action. I'm sick of talking."

"Look, catch yourself on. Sit down and tell me about it. My mum will make us a cup of good shipyard tea."

My mother, incredulous at the scene playing out before her, had been understandably quiet, bemused at the tragicomic events that were unfolding. She rose, taking my cue, "Yes, I'll make a wee cup of tea for youse." And she disappeared through the curtains that concealed the door to the scullery. Gradually Glenn calmed down until I gently released him from my grasp.

"Sit down mate." He sat down with a deep sigh of resignation.

"I'm sorry Tommy. It's not your fault. I could hardly control myself. I feel as if I'm going to explode. I'm at the end of my tether." The redness had gone from his face, along with the mask of anger and hate which had transformed his usually handsome appearance.

"I'm so pissed off Tommy, just one thing piling up on top of another. I felt smothered, doomed. It was building up like a pressure cooker. I'm afraid I'll kill somebody!"

"Next time you feel like that, come and see me."

He began to smile sheepishly, and then quietly laugh at himself.

"I'm a right bloody eejit, amn't I?"

My mum brought in the tea, shipyard stuff, strong and hot. The miraculous medicinal effect of tea throughout the ages has been amazing. Births, deaths, disasters, tea was the magic potion to concentrate minds and comfort distraught emotions.

"There you go son," clucked mum. "Glad to see you again. Things aren't as bad as you think. You take it easy now. Glenn, I'm going to bed. I'm sure you two men have things to talk about." She climbed the flight of stairs from the kitchen to the bedrooms upstairs. We could hear the ceiling creak as she moved around the room and finally all went quiet.

"Right Glenn, what's the craic? Why so violent?"

He took a slurp from the large mug mum had given him. "Ahhh, that's good. Better than all the Guinness in creation."

"I haven't seen you for ages Glenn. I thought you'd forgotten about me. It must be a year now."

"That was part of the problem Tommy. You were my mentor, always there in a crisis. Whenever I married Andrea, well, we became enamoured with each other. We intended to keep attending Fellowship, but with the engagement, then the marriage, changing job, God was sort of relegated. Imagine relegating the King of the Universe, He was way down our list of priorities. Then we have bad neighbours, two young guys who were partying to all hours. I knocked the door on a number of occasions and they couldn't have been nicer. But it went on, especially when they were off their heads with drugs and alcohol. One of them was connected, you know, paramilitaries, so I couldn't very well belt them, especially when I had witnessed my faith in Christ to them; but I have to tell you, those two don't realise how lucky they are. I could have choked them both. The spirit was restraining me."

"Aye, but you're under the influence of a different type of spirit tonight I'd say."

"Ye can say that again, I'm sorry Tommy."

"It's alright, go ahead."

"Then her ma and da were always interfering. You know what they thought of me. Andrea was too good for me; I was a guttersnipe. They only live in Orangefield. You'd think their house was the Taj Mahal. They tried to take over. They caused some terrible trouble between us.

Then my brother got worked over by a few yahoos in the Albert Bar. He was minding his own business and they picked on him and gave him a diggin'. I know who they are, Jim's quiet, he doesn't bother. They also know that I'm a Christian now, so I believe they took advantage. I was seething inside. I know the ringleader, a so-called hard man. I wouldn't have seen him in my way, he was terrified of me in the past. What does a Christian do? Every fibre of my being wanted revenge, God said 'No, vengeance is mine.' I found out where he lived, and on three occasions at different times, I waited on the scumbag coming home. Every time he didn't show."

"That was providence," I commented.

"Then there was work. I'm telling ya mate, I'm workin' on this building site. Ye know I'm a plasterer, and this big slabber, a brickie, starts pickin' on me. Every day for a week. Doin' wee stupid things like hiding my trowel or wee digs on the way past, playing to the gallery like. Then one day he went too far. I grabbed him by the throat. You should have heard him gurgle. Two guys had to pull me off him. I nearly lost my job. What a witness to Christ!

Anyway, after another row with Andrea, I threw the sofa up in the air, broke a few vases and thundered out. I was raging, like a ticking time bomb or a volcano about to explode. I was glaring at every man who passed me by. I swear if they'd looked sideways at me, I would have been down on their head. They'd be eating through a straw. I stalked up Dee Street and to the corner of the Newtownards Road. I'd thought about going into the Great Eastern, but realised too many people knew me in there; so, I made my way along the road, took a left at Templemore Avenue and crossed the Albertbridge Road to the Smoothing Iron.

On the way up Templemore Avenue, just past the Iron Hall on the left, a mob of yahoos were approaching. As they drew near, they went silent, they must have sensed danger. One was going to make a nasty comment and the leader abruptly shut him up. Every pore of my body must have exuded violence and menace. I would have been delighted if they'd done something. Their leader only nodded respectfully."

"What did you do then?"

"Well, I nodded back, belligerently. What can a man do when someone nods at them friendly like? It sort of disarms you, doesn't it?"

"So you went into the bar, "I urged. This is the gist of what followed.

"The bouncers on the door gave me a good hard look before stepping aside to let me in. Tuxedos and dicky bows are a bit pretentious for the Beersbridge Road I'd have thought! Anyway, they let me in. It was busy enough, but I found a place at the end of the bar, and started drinking, pints of Guinness and shots. A band was playing golden oldies mixed with modern stuff, two guitars and a keyboard. I was bombarded by this bloody awful noise and strobe lighting. It was terrible. Then this half naked wee girl came up to me, reeking of perfume and caked in make-up. She'd so much lipstick on if you'd tried to kiss her, you'd have slipped off! I gave her short shrift. The floor was filled with 'floosies', 'medallion men' and youngsters boppin' it out like nobody's business. The music was so loud you had to shout to be heard. Thump! Thump! Thump! It would have done your bloody head in! You couldn't hear yourself think. It was like all the devils dancing in Pandemonium.

Thank God there was a lull for a few minutes as the band had a toilet break. By this time the place was packed to the doors, groups of people sitting round tables, or squeezed into cubicles at the side; some guys standing in packs, laughing and flirting with semi-naked young girls, wearing either short skirts or long belts. It was hard to tell!

The band came back. By this time, I was seeing double, but, thank God, was not thinking 'single'. The leader stepped up to the microphone and asked for requests from the audience. I tried to be heard, but someone got in before me. The thunderous noise and manic gyrations started again and for what seemed ages; then stopped again.

Again I shouted at the top of my voice, "Play The Old Rugged Cross". The strident endless thumping began again, and I gradually struggled through the boiling cauldron of humanity until I reached the small raised stage where the band were playing. I virtually screamed at the leader "Play The Old Rugged Cross!", but it was impossible for anyone to hear anything amid the ear shattering babble of chaos.

I tried to grab one of the band leader's feet, but he got out of the way and kicked out. The music stopped abruptly. "Play The Old Rugged Cross you dickhead!" I hollered dodging the blows aimed at my head by the two guitarists, who were using their instruments as cudgels.

At last, I grabbed the leader's leg with one hand, and his shirt at the neck with the other, and threw him over my head into the bubbling melee of the now panic-stricken crowd. The other guitar player followed suit.

I felt hands being laid on me. Faces and bodies appeared for a moment, before disappearing back into the chaos from whence they had come. During this mayhem, all I could remember was shouting "The strength of Samson, Lord, the strength of Samson!" My feet went from under me, and a blur of fists and feet rained down on me. Then I was like a raft on a raging sea as I was literally born aloft by the bouncers and others and dumped unceremoniously on the pavement outside. I rose up, battered, bruised yet unbroken to confront the godless Philistine host. My clothes were in tatters. I tried to storm the citadel of the damned; the sturdy doors to the bar, guarded on the inside by the wary bouncers. Then breathing out threats and slaughter, shunned and given a wide berth by passers-by who steered clear of this obviously drunken nutter who wanted to fight the world, I made my way to your place.

So that's about it." He sighed apologetically." So, what happens now? Some Christian I am."

"Church militant on earth. The UVF would have sent you up to Connolly House with the jawbone of an ox!" I quipped. "I have a vision of you, a crusader knight, hacking your way through the Saracen ranks in a Holy Crusade."

"Very funny!" He smiled reluctantly.

"If you want my humble opinion?" I paused.

"I do," he said eagerly, leaning forward in the chair.

"Put God first, apologise. You and the wife go to counselling, and get back into the Fellowship. Oh! And take up crotchet or knitting!"

We talked into the wee small hours and quaffed a few more mugs of strong tea.

"It's time for me to make tracks. She'll be wondering where I am."

I left him to the door and watched him grow smaller as he walked up the street of Victorian terraced houses, hurriedly thrown up to house the poor who flooded into Belfast to meet the needs of the industrial expansion in the late nineteenth century.

In the distance he approached the end of the street which opened onto the Newtownards Road. On his left was the towering redbrick of Megain Memorial Presbyterian Church. On his right, the little church school built on the bombsite following two terrifying visits from the Luftwaffe during World War Two. The red brick buildings with their metal curving roofs were like a row of Nissen huts now used by the College of Further Education. Straight ahead, across the Newtownards Road, was a store called Crazy Prices, but only the large red capitals of Crazy, could be discerned from the bottom of the street. Above the store, a giant yellow crane rose like a mighty man, gently touched by the first fingers of the rosy sun of a beautiful dawn. Funnily enough, its name was Samson.

I laughed to myself, "Samson, the jawbone of an ox, church, industry and Philistines....Crazy! Just crazy!"

CHAPTER SEVEN

Granny Murphy Kicks the Bucket

Old Granny Murphy lay on a bed in a side ward of the Ulster Hospital at Dundonald. She was surrounded by her very large family, who crowded into the little room. Sons, daughters, nephews, nieces, grandchildren and great grandchildren waited in reverential anticipation as the old lady was gradually eased into eternity.

Suddenly, to everyone's amazement, she sat upright in the bed, and, in a firm and querulous voice demanded, "Where's our Joe?"

"We don't know mum. We haven't heard from him for ages," soothed Lottie, her eldest daughter, taking her hand and stroking it.

The wizened matriarch abruptly pulled her hand away and held it up, skeletal and trembling before her eyes, as she pronounced 'terrible imprecations' on the unfortunate absent Joe.

"He never came to see me when I was alive! I don't want him at my funeral. He's a good for nothin' rapscallion!"

Breathing out threatenings and slaughter upon the head of poor Joe, she 'kicked the bucket' with a metaphorical "clang", and, hopefully, passed over to a better world.

Three days later, the Reverend William Kilpatrick, minister of Queen's Island Presbyterian Church in Mersey Street, was just finishing his breakfast in the manse in the leafy suburb of Belmont. His two children

had just left for school, and he was enjoying a final cup of tea before commencing his pastoral duties for the day.

"I've to officiate at the Murphy funeral today. Old Florrie is to be buried in Roselawn," he commented offhandedly to his wife who was busy at the sink.

"Births, weddings and deaths. You're a hatch, match and dispatch man, dear," joked Fiona, over the sound of clattering crockery. "You do it so well."

"It's awkward. The family hardly ever attend church. They're a rough crowd. The police are never away from their door."

"Is the funeral from the church or the funeral parlour?"

"Neither. It's from her home in Redcliffe Street."

"That's going to be a crush, isn't it?"

"Immediate family, I suppose, and relatives inside. Friends and well-wishers smoking and quietly chatting outside."

"Most people on our books have no interest in God," Fiona complained. "It's a sort of, well, Presbyterian Paganism, if there can be such a thing!"

"In this land we usually receive our labels at birth, Cultural Christianity it's called," he smiled grimly. "Anyway love, I should be back in a couple of hours. A short sermon at the house followed by an even shorter sermon at the cemetery. Pretty normal stuff. Just make a few sandwiches for lunch will you Fiona?"

He kissed her lightly on the cheek. She followed him to the door and waved as he steered the gleaming black Mercedes out of the drive and into the tree lined avenue. The waving foliage was mirrored on the car's sleek bodywork.

When he arrived in Redcliffe Street, the black hearse was already there, but a space had been reserved for him near the house in the narrow thoroughfare. This was part of the old area of 'two up, two down, outside toilet in the backyard' houses. The gantries used to build Titanic and her sister ships, Olympic and Britannic, had been demolished in the early seventies. Now two towering cranes dominated the Belfast skyline, and straddled what was once the biggest dry dock on earth.

A redevelopment plan was underway, and much of the maze of huddled streets had already been demolished. As new social housing gradually emerged, a slow exodus from the east was taking place, as the population flowed to the burgeoning new estates in Dundonald, Holywood, Bangor, Newtownards, and even further afield.

The little house was crammed with immediate family. Daughters and granddaughters sobbed quietly as they recalled the life of so dominant a figure in this matriarchal society. It was the women who were the lynchpins of community; who raised their children and made ends meet; while the men, full of machismo, philosophised in bars, and generally 'hung their fiddles at the door'. The wives and mothers were the beating heart of family life. Most slaved in poorly paid menial jobs to augment their husband's poor, or squandered, wages; and kept the ever-present skulking wolves of poverty and hunger from the door.

The open coffin was supported by two trestles in the living room. The minister took his place at the head. Through the window to his right the black hearse loomed ominously. To his left, a little back room was filled with family, as was the scullery beside it. To his right and front, a narrow flight of stairs ascended to two small bedrooms, and further to the right, a long glass door trimmed with wood gave access to the small hall which exited immediately onto the pavement outside. Every space was filled with grieving family.

The proceedings could not have run smoother. The Reverend Kilpatrick had hardly known Florrie Murphy, but had gleaned information, and some humorous anecdotes from family and friends. He had completed the tribute, a resumé of Florrie's life. He was halfway through his sermon when there was a kerfuffle, and loud voices outside the door.

"The Lord died to bring reconciliation and harmony between God and man," the Reverend Kilpatrick preached.

"Let me in!" snarled a male voice.

"Take yerself off, ye worthless git!" a growling reply.

"Between the nations, communities and families," continued the Reverend.

"She didn't want you near the place!"

"Hey! Take it easy!"

"Who the hell do ya think yer pushin'?"

A cacophony of strident voices filled the air.

"Let him in. He's her son too," protested a crone.

"As we remember Florence, let us consider the transience of our own lives in the light of eternity," continued the Reverend William, uncomfortably.

The door burst open and a burly, tough looking individual, reeking of alcohol, wrestled his way into the middle of the living room.

"I want to see my ma!" he wailed. "And nobody's goin' to stop me."

"Get out! Get out! Ye stinkin' git!" shouted a very large woman sporting a Mohican hairstyle, and flashing dark blue and red tattoos on both exposed, and ample, arms. She moved towards the interloper with a speed that belied her bulk, and like a Ballymacarrett Boudicca, hit him on the chin with a straight right that Muhammed Ali would have been proud of. He careered backwards into the door. The glass shattered. Chaos ensued as scuffling and fighting erupted and punches were thrown.

The two employees from Brown's Funeral Parlour, paid to see to the dead, struggled through buffetings and blows, and succeeded in preventing the coffin from being knocked over. With valiant determination, they were able to screw down the coffin lid, and, with great difficulty, dexterously manoeuvre Florrie outside. Covered by the driver, they managed to shove the coffin unceremoniously into the back of the hearse as hand-to-hand combat spilled onto the street.

The arrival of Joe had been the catalyst to ignite old simmering resentments and smouldering hatreds among the family. Some brave neighbours attempted to break up the combatants, but in vain. The place was in uproar.

Hats were knocked off; people were knocked over; dresses and lips were split, and blood spilt. As two men fought, a woman came from behind one and hit him over the head with her high heeled shoe. Women were pulling each other's hair as they rolled on the ground. Another man in a pin striped suit was clobbered with a wreath, sending a little shower of flower petals into the air.

Thankfully, someone had 'phoned the police, who, after what seemed an interminable time, turned up in a Landover and an unmarked car. Gradually order was restored. Collars were straightened, hats picked up and repositioned, shirts tucked in and nose bleeding stemmed, until a semblance of dignity returned to the assembled mourners. After six uniformed constables had, with great difficulty, restrained and bundled two particularly pugnacious belligerents into the back of the Landrover, 'peace came dropping slow'.

One was the hapless Joe. His face was battered, his clothes tattered. He looked like a refugee from a 'Rocky' movie. He was driven away, still shouting defiantly at those who had barred him from his own mother's funeral.

A delegation was quickly chosen from the family to attend the interment ceremony at Roselawn. All went well, without any more drama, as the coffin was lowered into the open grave. The Reverend Kilpatrick closed the short graveside oration with the prayer of committal.

"Now we come to commit the body of our dear departed sister Florence Murphy to the grave. Earth to earth. Ashes to ashes. Dust to dust. In the sure and certain hope of the resurrection of our Lord Jesus Christ. Amen."

"Thank God for that!" The reverend offered his own silent prayer to the Almighty. It was with a great sense of relief that he climbed into the car and made for home.

"For goodness sake! What happened to you?" cried Fiona, as he entered the kitchen and laid his Bible on the table.

"Did someone take exception to your preaching dad? At long last!" teased his son David mischievously. "What a shiner! I've been wanting to do that for years!"

"You've got a split lip too!" gasped his daughter Lisa.

"Your collar has blood on it! You have been in the wars!" exclaimed Fiona.

"It was one big chaotic brawl, and I was trapped in the middle of it," he explained earnestly. "I was trying to break up the fighting and kept being hit more by accident than intention. It was wild."

He was very sombre and serious until he saw his family attempt to smother their laughter behind their hands.

"Church militant on earth dad. Pike in thatch and all that. I warned you that these undertakers are all professional boxers," joked David with mock concern.

"Very funny," answered the Reverend Kilpatrick.

Then the whole family erupted into uncontrollable laughter.

CHAPTER EIGHT

The Good Turn

Lennie closed the door of his house in a backstreet of the city. It was one of a long row of two up two down terrace houses. They had recently been refurbished and fitted with bathrooms, inside toilets and hot water; as part of a rehabilitation scheme carried out by the local Housing Executive.

His car was parked about seven feet away next to the edge of the pavement. It was brand new and sparkled in the early morning sun. He was paying it off by instalments. He noticed immediately the damage; a wing mirror lay on the pavement. He quickly looked at the other side. A wing mirror lay on the roadway. He was furious. Someone had vandalised his car, sometime during the night, or in the early hours of the morning. There were a good number of cars in the street, but only his had been touched; so it wasn't a crowd of teenagers, he deduced.

"Who could it have been?" He went over the events of the past week in his mind, eliminating possible situations that could have led someone to do this. Was it retaliation? Revenge? Jealousy? He flicked through his memory like a clerk would through folders on a computer.

"Eureka! That scumbag McGowan!" He recalled his own sarcastic comments in the local bar when he'd joked that McGowan should close his mouth because there was a draft; and later on, that he was so ugly he made Quasimodo look like Sean Connery. The all-male company had laughed, but Lennie knew that McGowan was livid. His eyes were full of hate behind the feigned smile. "It must have been him," Lennie concluded decisively. "It must have been."

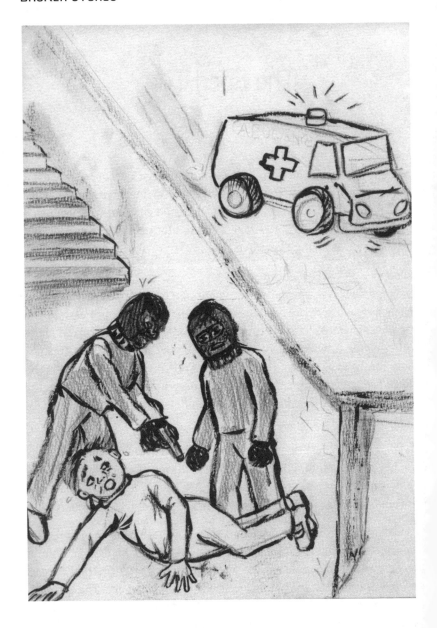

Later that night Lennie violently kicked open the door of a second-floor apartment two streets away from where he lived. The block was a new build, and privately owned by the occupants. McGowan was not at home, so Lennie proceeded to wreck the flat and its furnishings with great gusto. He brandished a baseball bat like a possessed berserker in a Viking war party. In a frenzy, he smashed the TV set, computer, adjoining windows, glass fronted cabinets and anything of value. The inside of the flat was a chaotic mess; sacked and devastated by this breathless destroyer.

As he ran downstairs, he pushed two residents out of his way and ducked out the door. He jumped into his car and roared into the middle of the street. He had to brake suddenly to avoid a small child about to retrieve his ball. A mother quickly snatched the child out of harm's way, and glared ominously at Lennie. The car snarled down the street, and away in a cloud of exhaust.

"You really are some pup!" commented the tall, athletic man he had come to see. His hair was black and wiry; his nose, slightly aquiline, surmounted by two deep set dark brown eyes. His features resembled those of a Barbary pirate. He was dressed simply in a blue checked shirt and blue jeans, held up by a broad brown belt.

"You are in soapy bubble, I mean, trouble, mate. Our, shall we call them, competitors, are anxious to interview you. It was wise you never went home last night. Of course, they know it was you. You didn't even wear a mask, and of course you had to drive that big flashy car. You might as well have left a calling card."

"I was ragin'. I just didn't think."

"Aye, yer good at that aren't ye? Not thinkin' I mean."

Lennie said nothing, but dropped his head onto his chest.

"I'm reluctant to make any 'phone calls. The line's probably bugged. I've a guy doing his best for you. Go away into the kitchen there and make us both a cuppa."

Lennie filled the electric kettle with water, fetched two mugs from a shelf above the sideboard, and dropped teabags into each. He noticed that he was shaking, and though he presented a brave face, inside his stomach was churning with terror. These people were out to 'whack' him. He thought of his parents and wider family; his grieving mother weeping over his coffin; a minister speaking at the graveside; rain dripping from umbrellas, and the smell of flowers.

He'd joined the 'organisation' in his teens, due to peer pressure rather than some high-flown political ideology. If you didn't enjoy the protection of the group, you were vulnerable, a potential victim to every bully and loudmouth in the area. He had hung around on the periphery of the action. He kept his head down and paid his dues. In fact, for the past couple of years, he may as well not have been a member.

He groaned. "Why the hell did I do that?" Now he was up to his neck in it, a swamp with no way out.

"What about the bloody tea?"

He was jolted from his regrets, and switched off the violently bubbling kettle.

They sat opposite each other at a small desk near the window. Lennie could hear the distant mumble and growl of incessant traffic on the main road outside. As they finished their tea, a door opened, and a small, lean, rip cord of a man entered. He had a few days growth of stubble on his face. His eyes were blue, and his hair greying. He ignored Lennie, and spoke to John.

"I've done my best. I've been running round like a whore at a hockey match. I saw McGuirk and McGaw. They negotiated with the 'Philistines', and they've reached a deal."

"Well, Tommy, spit it out."

"He's to report to Headquarters at seven o' clock tonight."

"What are they going to do with me?" asked an apprehensive, and still shaking, Lennie.

"They're givin' him a choice." Tommy went on, still ignoring Lennie.

"What do ya mean?" interrupted Lennie.

"A beating with baseball bats, or a bullet through the leg."

"You must be joking!" gasped a horrified Lennie.

"Take it easy son," soothed John. "Would you rather have a bullet through your brain? They've left it to us because you're one of us."

"Otherwise you'd be goin' fer yer tea," Tommy pointed his finger like a gun at the young man's head.

"I only wrecked the bastard's flat. He broke the wing mirrors off my car," complained Lennie.

"Well, it's a good job he was out when you called," commented John. "He just happens to be connected; right to the top."

"Wing mirrors!" exclaimed Tommy. "They'd be cutting yer bloody ears off, among other things, before they stiffed ya, ye bloody eejit!" He shook his head and smiled grimly.

"Look at it this way Lennie," John smiled. "They're doin' you a good turn."

"A good turn!" gulped Lennie.

"A lesser of two evils son. At least yer ma can visit you in hospital, not in the cemetery," encouraged John.

"Where are they going to do it?" asked the potential victim resignedly.

"The nearest spare ground or back entry probably," explained Tommy. "Don't worry, they'll 'phone for an ambulance before it's done."

"That's reassuring," shrugged Lennie.

"Sure look on the bright side lad. You can always put a claim in," quipped John. The two men laughed quietly to themselves.

The late news reported that a young man, in his early twenties, had been shot in the leg near the city centre; in a suspected paramilitary punishment shooting. He was taken to the Ulster Hospital, where his condition was non-life-threatening.

After he left hospital, Lennie, acting on the advice from friends, moved to another area of the city. He found out, a few months later, that McGowan had not vandalised his car after all. An old girlfriend, a year back, still simmering from the pain of a broken relationship, had attacked the wing mirrors of his precious car.

CHAPTER NINE

A Ripping Yarn

The changing room smelt of an overpowering combination of Wintergreen and sweat as the various boxers warmed up. They shadow boxed, skipped or punched their trainers' heavy gloves in preparation for their oncoming bouts.

Jackie Griffin was a sight to behold. Resplendent in tight fitting red shorts with a white stripe down the outside, a white vest and shiny boxing boots, he punched the air at an imaginary opponent.

He looked like a chunky Italian Romeo. He was stocky, with a well-developed physique. His darkly handsome face was surmounted by a mane of black wavy hair that was combed to perfection. He was a welder by trade, having served an apprenticeship in Harland and Wolff shipyard. Now in his mid-twenties, he stood five feet ten inches tall, a wonderful specimen of Belfast macho manhood. Affable and popular among his peers, he sang cabaret in the pubs and clubs of the city. He was nicknamed 'Tom Jones'; Jackie loved the ladies, and the ladies loved Jackie. Reared in the east of the city, Jackie had had to fight to hold his own, and found that he had a useful pair of hands; so he was encouraged to box at the local amateur club, Ledley Hall.

Stuffer Kane and Herbie Young were his trainers until Stuffer quit through ill health, and Herbie ran the club alone. Herbie was a gentleman. He had been a useful amateur in his day, and had a love of the noble sport. He was a salesman in the Gas Department, who had a love of literature, and would always quote Shaw or Shakespeare. His influence on young men in that troubled area during the conflict was positive and profound, even though he had

lost his mother to an IRA bomb in the city centre. He steered young men and lads away from shadowy organisations, and into sport and other constructive pursuits.

Herbie held his gloved hands up while Jackie proceeded to energetically punch them.

"Keep your right hand up when you throw the left. Don't drop the right or you'll be a sucker for a left hook. Good. Good. Straight left. Set your opponent up and let the big right hand loose."

They stopped, and Jackie limbered up by touching his toes.

"Those shorts are very tight Jackie. Are you sure you sure you're going to be alright?" asked Herbie shaking his head.

"Aye, they'll be great. They're really comfortable. You worry too much Herbie."

"It's a wonder you're not speaking with a squeaky voice," smiled Herbie.

Jackie climbed into the ring to loud acclaim from his fans, many of them ladies who had come to support him. He acknowledged the applause by raising his hands, and kept warm by shadow boxing in and around his corner.

His opponent, Jim Neill from Lisburn Boxing Club, entered the ring to a roar of encouragement from his followers. He also acknowledged the crowd by raising his hands and bounced up and down on the balls of his feet to keep warm. Jackie was a little disconcerted when he noticed that Neill had a mane of blonde hair to rival his own black thatch.

The referee, dressed all in white, called the two combatants into the centre of the ring.

"I want a good clean fight. Defend yourself at all times. No hitting below the belt. Break quickly when you're told. Best of luck to you both. Shake hands and come out fighting."

The boxers joined gloves and went back to their respective corners to await the bell that would signal the opening of hostilities. The bell rang. As Jim Neill stepped away from his corner, his trainer gently pulled the mop of flowing blonde hair away from his head, revealing a shaved dome that gleamed in the powerful lights above the ring. The audience gasped; then laughter rippled through the building.

The boxers squared up, moving cautiously around the ring as they probed for each other's weaknesses. Very few blows were struck as the fighters continued to weigh each other up. Near the end of the first round, laughter broke out again, just before the bell sounded for the break.

Jackie hurried back to his corner and sat down on the portable stool. Herbie rubbed Jackie's sweating face with the magic sponge.

"This is goin' great," enthused Jackie. "They're all laughing at his baldy head."

"No, they're not laughing at his baldy head Jackie. They're laughing at your sausage and two veg!"

Jackie looked down in horror. His pants had ripped revealing all the 'family jewels'. Mortification registered on his handsome face, which had now turned pale. He pulled his knees together and used his hands as cover. Herbie sent his other cornerman to the dressing room to sequester another pair of shorts.

The unfortunate Jim Skellin, another Ledley Hall boxer who was next on the card, was unceremoniously deprived of his breeches, and left abandoned on a bench. The others raced back to Jackie's corner again, where they provided a human screen while the hapless Romeo changed. The crowd hooted, whistled, mocked and laughed good naturedly as the transformation took place.

When all had settled down, the bell rang for the second round. Jackie hardly struck a blow for the rest of the fight. His embarrassment was intense, especially as he noticed some of his beautiful admirers in the crowd. It was with some relief that Jackie walked back to the corner at the end of the fight to be consoled and comforted by Herbie, and Big Al, his cornerman. He lost the fight by a narrow margin.

As he emerged from the shower and dried himself off with a rough towel, he apologised.

"I'm sorry I lost, Herbie. I just lost all concentration after that.... incident."

"We're here to give you a 'debriefing'," joked Big Al.

"Very funny! Very funny!" spat Jackie.

"Don't worry Jackie," remarked Herbie. "It could have been worse. I suppose you could call it a 'split decision'!"

Jackie threw the towel at his head.

CHAPTER TEN

Death of a Sparrow

"Your father has only a few months, or even weeks, to live!"

His mother intercepted him before he entered the little kitchen house in the tough working-class area. Her face was full of sorrow and anxiety. A tear glistened at the corner of her eye.

"That's what the consultant said."

She had been a once beautiful woman but a hard, tough existence had taken its physical and mental toll.

It was a late summer afternoon. The incessant grumble of rush hour traffic could be heard thirty yards away where the side street met the main Albertbridge Road.

The sky was blue and the heat, though luxuriant, was trapped in the maze of narrow streets making the atmosphere cloying and oppressive. Pigeons, comically waddling "street pickers", heads nodding up and down, hurriedly consumed the morsels of bread thrown out on their behalf. The flock of industrial rock doves, startled by a passing car, rose together in a frenzy of beating wings and made for the safety of chimney tops, sloping blue slate roofs and gutters.

It had been a fine satisfying day at college. He had especially enjoyed the illustrated lectures on Education and the Arts. It fascinated him how faith in the Absolute had been manifest in every aspect of human existence. Literature, painting, sculpture and architecture had all reflected the awe of eternity. His intellect had

been stimulated by photographs of ancient ruins. The churches, mosques, pyramids and ziggurats towered like great colossi throughout human civilisation.

Now, confronted with his mother's tragic news, a feeling of nausea arose in the pit of his stomach. Crushing dread and disappointment traumatised his emotions and drove out all the pleasurable memories of the day.

He did not know what to say or feel. He was embarrassed as his mother laid her grey head on his shoulder and wept quietly. The situation was awkward. He was unable to cope with this rare and raw show of emotion.

"He doesn't know, son. Don't tell him. We'll try and let him enjoy what's left of his life," she reasoned.

He felt panic stricken, trapped. Where to go? How to escape? Nowhere to go. Nowhere to escape.

"OK Mum," he half-heartedly put his arm around her. "Whatever you say."

At the other end of the street, terraced uniformly on both sides, the Presbyterian church soared skyward in red brick, its steeple an indicator of other worlds beyond. Behind the shops on the Newtownards Road, Goliath, one of the huge shipyard cranes, reared upward; a towering sentinel that bestrode the massive dry dock. He stood resplendent and clear, his yellow paint radiant in sunlight, contrasting with white cirrus clouds. The scene was a huge watercolour shaped by an unseen hand.

"Funny how a crisis heightens perception," he thought. "Things only half noticed are brought into focus. What was only a subconscious blur becomes clearly defined, especially under the microscope of tragedy. Everything becomes more substantial, more solid and more real. From a distant panoramic sweep of hills to a pattern on a tablecloth."

They stepped from the street into the tiny hall and opened a glass door which gave access to a small living room. Immediately to the right, a gap in the wall was covered by a long heavy curtain. Behind this, a flight of narrow stairs, centrally carpeted, rose steeply up to two bedrooms. The more spacious, dominated by a double bed to the left of a large window which overlooked the street, was his parents' room. The curtains, suspended from a rail, flanked the window. At the top was a roller blind with a hanging cord which could be pulled down to provide privacy.

His smaller back room was to the right at the top of the stairs. His window looked onto the backs of houses from a parallel street. Their backyards were separated by a narrow alleyway where dustbins were placed outside back doors on bin collection day.

His father sat on an old battered armchair. He was wearing a white shirt open at the collar. With relief he had shed the dark coat of his 'Sunday best' suit after arriving back from the hospital. Gratefully he had flopped down exhausted on the chair. He had turned on the television set which sat on the four-legged table under the front window.

"I'll put the dinner on, Harry," mumbled his wife as she walked quickly into the scullery.

"Well dad, how's it going?" he asked as matter of factly as he could.

"Tired son, very tired, but over all not too bad," replied Harry. "As my old mother used to say 'Another shirt'll do me'."

"You never know da. Maybe you'll get a telegram from the queen," he lied.

"Not a chance son. A lot o' mates I grew up with are gone like flowers that die in the Autumn," Harry mused. "When the Almighty calls we gotta go. 'Come in number seventy-seven, your time is up!' Sure I was at Johnny Brigg's funeral last week. We served our time together in the Sirocco Works as engineers. Sirocco means big wind. That suited Johnny, God rest him. He never shut up!"

Tom's mother had created a dilemma for Tom. Do you lie to a dying man? Tell him everything's alright? Where's the morality in that, or tell him the truth so he can prepare for whatever lies ahead? He felt compromised, dishonest.

On the other hand, by telling someone of their impending death, would you snatch away hope and hasten the approach of 'The Stranger'?

"Are you not goin' to sit down for a while?" His father indicated the sofa positioned under the bannisters of the staircase.

"Well, I was thinking of calling on Davey Hamilton about the Youth Club."

"What about your dinner?" called his mum from the scullery. She had been avidly listening to every word of their conversation. "It's nearly ready."

"Sure it's five o' clock. You'll be interrupting his tea," protested Harry.

"I'm not really hungry mum. I'll see you later dad."

Tom stumbled out as quickly as he could into the warm summer evening. He was relieved to escape the intolerable atmosphere of emotional stress that tongue-tied and almost paralysed him. Yet he was riddled with guilt at his moral cowardice.

After having walked for miles around the east of the city, he ended up at the Presbyterian church at the bottom of the street. The Youth Club was in full swing in the church halls. Two table tennis tables had been setup, and games were underway. Modern music blared and filled the place. Young people were busy throwing darts, playing chess or Monopoly at tables positioned around the hall. The incessant rumble and periodic thumps of a five a side football match could be heard from the large hall above.

A middle-aged man, thin, clean shaved, of average height and short cropped hair, presided over the scene. He wore casual trousers and a red pullover, with a whistle draped around his neck. He mouthed something at Tom, but his voice was completely overwhelmed by the din. He blew his whistle. Its sound triumphed and everyone looked his way.

"Turn the music down!" he shouted.

"What?"

"Turn the music down!" Exasperated, he walked over to the CD player and turned down the volume.

"Oh!" two girls exclaimed.

"Yes ladies," he laughed, shaking his head. "Keep it down a bit, OK."

He turned to Tom, "you look a bit forlorn, like somebody stole the froth off your pint of Guinness. Let's go into the sanctuary and talk."

He led Tom through the minister's office, carpeted in blue with a large varnished oak desk, and lined with shelves heavy with books. The auditorium was covered in the same Presbyterian blue carpet. They walked silently down a side aisle towards the back of the church and sat down in one of the many oak varnished pews.

Tom looked towards the front of the building. The pulpit took centre stage. An open Bible, a large ponderous tome, occupied a small lectern at the front of the pulpit. This signified the pre-eminence of the word of God over the church and tradition. It was the 'regulative principle' which established doctrine and guided behaviour.

A blue cloth hung from the front of the pulpit. On it, in red and yellow, was depicted 'The Burning Bush', the symbol of Presbyterianism. Moses in the wilderness was confronted by a burning bush, burning but unconsumed, from which issued the voice of God.

The architectural style was minimalist, plain and understated, free of idols, icons and statues; an example of what someone called 'the culturally threadbare coat of Scottish Calvinism'. The only concession to any hint of 'indulgence' were the beautifully coloured arched stained-glass windows set in the walls.

"You've got a face on you like John Knox!" smiled Norman, referring to the father of the Protestant Reformation in Scotland, whose mentor had been burned at the stake, and who had been a slave for years in French galleys. It was said of Knox that 'he neither feared nor flattered flesh'. "Well mate, what's your problem?" continued Norman.

"The doctors say my dad has a few months, more likely weeks to live."

"Good heavens!" exclaimed Norman. "No wonder you're depressed."

"Mum doesn't want to tell him. I don't feel right about that. To be honest, I don't know what to do. I mean, how do you handle it?"

"You don't handle it mate. You just go through it. Like the song says 'One day at a time sweet Jesus'," advised Norman.

"I just found out today. My mum needs me but all I want to do is run away and hide somewhere."

"It's understandable son. All I can say is that by the grace of God you'll get what you need when you need it." He went quiet for a moment and rubbed his chin slowly with his hand.

"Look Tom, the family and I are going to Scotland for a few weeks. I have a greenhouse in the back garden, and I need someone to water the tomatoes every few days while I'm away. I can give you the key to my place, and you can go there anytime you like, so you can get your head showered and take a break. Just like a place of refuge and prayer. You know what I mean?"

"That would be great Norman," enthused Tom.

"The only condition is that you don't have wild drunken orgies with wicked women dancing on the dining room table with roses between their teeth," ribbed Norman.

"What about selling your furniture while you're away?"

"That's settled then. You can come back with me later and I'll show you what opens what. OK?"

"OK Norman. That's fine."

They walked back to the hall. He had attended Sunday School here as a child.

"What is man's chief end?" Miss Maize addressed a ring of little boys sitting on foldaway wooden chairs. Tom's hand shot up. "Man's chief end is to glorify God and enjoy him forever," he parroted. "Well done Tom. You really know your catechism," she smiled and gave him a 'penny chew'.

Most of the fighting was done after Sunday School as boys engaged in single combat in the arena of the toilets; a training ground for the up-and-coming church militant on earth.

His father's condition deteriorated over the following weeks. He seemed to waste away, gradually collapsing from the inside, deflating like an air bag. He found it difficult to walk and then was confined to bed.

He had been a barroom philosopher, whose wisdom and wit were sought after and admired. An active man, he loved to socialise in the local pubs on the Newtownards Road. It was heart-breaking to watch his decline. Fewer and fewer friends came to see him as he slowly faded from this earth.

Life went on. Tom wanted the world to stop. He wanted to scream "Can't you see what's happening here? My dad is dying."

Mocking his frustration, the world moved on. Sunrise and sunset, day and night; inexorably turning from the beginning of time until its inevitable end.

He arrived home from college one afternoon to find his dad sitting on the bottom step of the stairs. He was dressed only in his shirt. His skin was pallid, tissue paper stretched tightly over bone. The little hair on his balding head was dishevelled. He was exhausted and breathing hard. He could not speak but just beckoned with his hand signifying the futility of his situation.

"For God's sake dad, what are you playing at? What are you trying to prove?!" scolded Tom.

His white legs were thin and bony poking out from under his shirt which hardly covered his private parts. Tom gently picked him up and carried him like a child slowly upstairs, just as his father had carried him all those years ago. He was shocked at how light he was. He put him down gently on the bed.

"You can't do this anymore dad. You can't." He almost wept.

"I'm dying son. I'm dying," his father whispered. "I've known since the hospital. You and your mother tried to keep it from me, but I know."

Tom sat on the edge of the bed. He saw his father and himself reflected in the long mirror set into the wardrobe in that small room with the floral wallpaper. How grotesque it was; nightmarish and unbelievably painful.

He hugged his dad and felt the stubble like sandpaper on his cheek. Then he laid him against the propped-up pillows. He looked down on the balding head above the sunken eyes and emaciated cheeks. He was like a prisoner in an extermination camp; and the only liberation for him was death. It was approaching, slowly, surely, mercilessly.

Tom bent over his dad again. "Alright son, alright. I love you son. Don't worry." He felt his dad's dried lips kiss him on the cheek, and his hand pat his shoulder in consolation.

Tom wanted to yell and scream at the injustice of it all. What the hell was God doing anyway? As he held his father he wanted to weep, sob and cry out all his sorrow and frustration and love. He wanted to say "Daddy, I love you. I'm so sorry I undervalued you and took you for granted. Oh Daddy! Forgive me! Please forgive me!"

Of course, he did none of these things, but simply, with great care, detached himself from his father and softly said "I love you too dad. Mum will be home soon." He negotiated the narrow stairs, sat down on the sofa and wept.

Norman's house indeed proved to be a welcome place of refuge. The semi-detached was situated in the Ballyhackamore area. The dwellings here were mainly privately owned. It was a typical middle-class suburb with gardens front and back. The avenues were quiet, pleasant and tree lined. It was a delightful green leafy land, in contrast to the tough concrete warren from which he came.

He let himself in the front door into the large hallway, passed the parlour on the right, through the living room and kitchen and into the well-tended back garden. The greenhouse was at the bottom right-hand corner, in the angle where two hedges met. As he entered, he was immediately conscious of the pungent smell of tomatoes on the vine. Lovely bright red glistening orbs were set against the dark green foliage under the sloping glass panes of a tentlike roof.

He was totally ignorant of horticulture. The only greenery Tom was accustomed to was groundsel growing out of the backyard wall. As the foliage crowded the stalks, he took biblical advice. Those which bore no fruit he broke off. Those which did he purged so they might bear more fruit. The results were startling as the tomatoes burgeoned and proliferated.

He filled a large blue watering can from a freestanding tap at the back door, and watched as the pure soft water from the Silent Valley in the Mourne Mountains cascaded over the thirsty plants.

It was here in this citadel of solace that he wet the leaves with his tears.

At first he pleaded with the Almighty to work a miracle and heal his father. When the latter's condition got worse, he guiltily prayed for his dad's suffering to be at an end soon. His mind was full of memories of the man who held him as a child, and tucked him into bed; or who took him by the hand among the tall elegant swans languishing at the water's edge in Victoria Park. The one who took him on his knee at suppertime. Dressed in his grimy dungarees, smelling of Guinness and industry, his father fed him from his plate. He would quote from memory the poems of Robert Service, and he knew Grey's Elegy by heart. Due to this literary osmosis, Tom could never forget many of the lines.

But then there was the man that Tom hated. The man who drank too much and was popular in the bar, but who 'hung his fiddle at the door'. The black cloud that descended and threatened a coming storm.

He recalled the nights when a storm rattled the window panes and moaned around the eaves and chimneys; when rain filled the Lagan Basin like a thick curtain of mist. The wind wailed a banshee threnody through wires and shipyard cranes and gantries and the deluge drenched the maze of slanted blue-slate rooftops. Water streamed down spouts from overflowing gutters and gurgled incessantly in gratings at the edge of the streets.

The house was filled with strident angry voices. Upstairs in bed, his body was as taut and stiff as a corpse. He clutched the bedclothes and stopped his ears to his mammy's screams for help. Bruised sore, loathing self, aching yet in dreams, heard the distant breaking delft of fragile things.

Tom answered the door. There stood a little boy of about seven years old. He was dressed in khaki shorts, plimsols and a grubby grey shirt stained with food.

"I found him in the yard Tommy. He can't fly. My mammy told me to bring him to you. Can you help him?" he blurted. He looked up eagerly, his dark eyes shining and full of hope under a curtain of black hair. He offered a little bird in a small brown cardboard box. "He can't fly Tommy. My mammy said you could help him. Can you Tommy? Can you?" he pleaded breathlessly.

"Settle down Timmy, settle down. Let's have a look." Tommy soothed. It was a fledgling house sparrow, fallen from the nest.

He took the bird with great difficulty from the box and gently overcame its feeble protestations. He could feel its little heart pulsate frantically against his fingers. It was terrified. How could this delicate fragile thing, its tiny heart hammering in a frenzy, know that his intentions toward it were good. How could it possibly conceive that Timmy had rescued it from rats, cats and other predators that stalked the darkness.

Timmy followed Tom through the living room into the scullery where he put the little bird back in the box with a few crumbs of bread and a saucer of fresh water.

"Well Timmy, that's about as much as we can do for him, mate. Come back tomorrow and see how he is. OK?"

"Thanks Tommy," Timmy smiled. As they passed through the living room Harry coughed hoarsely. Timmy stopped. "My mammy told me yer daddy's sick Tommy. My daddy was sick too last year but he died. He used to make me laugh so much Tommy. My mammy misses him too. I'll pray yer daddy gets well."

"Thanks Timmy." Tommy smiled down at the wee fella, one who had lived such a short time and suffered so much. After his father's death, his mother lost the will to live. Her heart broke. Poor Timmy was neglected, and but for his granny who looked after him, and saw that he was clothed and fed and attended school, he probably would have gone into care.

His mother responded to counselling, and improved somewhat. She still suffered from periodic bouts of chronic depression. Once she had over dosed. It was a desperate Timmy, dirty face streaming with tears, who had sounded the alarm and saved her life.

The college Tom attended was situated among the leafy suburbs of south Belfast. Built on a hill, it was surrounded by beautifully tended copses of trees, interspersed with marvellous gardens with flaming flowers and various shades of green shrubs.

"How can anybody maintain that this happened by accident?" declared Stephen. The question was rhetorical, as he surveyed with pleasure the splendour which surrounded them as they descended the hill towards the large iron gates of the imposing entrance.

Stephen was a fellow English student, and President of the college Christian Union. They had both just left a lecture on Shakespearean tragedy.

Tom began, "How can God permit such horror? He lets an old mad fool like King Lear trigger the descent into murder and moral chaos. Then there's Othello, the big dope, manipulated by evil Iago; and MacBeth, enticed by his wife to usurp the throne and murder good decent Duncan."

"Well, it shows sin has its consequences," commented Stephen, a small dapper lad from the suburbs, who wore designer gear, and whose car was parked at the bottom of the hill. The grounds were a riot of colour under an azure sky. The river Lagan could be seen winking and sparkling in the distance. The whole of creation was showing off, strutting its stuff like a beautiful sensuous woman on a catwalk.

"Is Shakespeare questioning the nature of God, even his very existence?" continued Tom. "The gods they mock us for their sport. Life is the slobbering idiot's tale "full of sound and fury and signifying nothing"."

"True, but order returns to the universe again," interrupted Stephen. "Sanity returns after madness. Anyway, Shakespeare's over-rated. Tolstoy had no time for him at all. He thought his plots ridiculous."

"But why do the innocent suffer. Is God a sadist; a cosmic Caligula? Is he an experimenter with rats in a maze? Or are there two gods of equal power, one good, one evil, vying for control?" Tom argued.

"God is both almighty and good. He became human to die for humans. He was the innocent sufferer who hung in the darkness. All you are doing Thomas, is echoing the 'Why?' of the great answerer himself. God doesn't give us a reasoned argument for the problem of pain, but an historic reference point. Truth is not an "-ism" or philosophy. Truth is a person."

"Well preached reverend," retorted Tom sharply. "It's all very well spouting scripture. It's a different matter when you're going through it."

"We all go through it in this world Thomas. Everyone does. There's no escape."

"But's what the point?" asked Tom emphatically.

"That's where faith comes in. Either all this beauty, complexity, glory, striving, suffering and death is a complete meaningless absurdity, or 'not a sparrow falls to the ground unless the heavenly Father wills it'. Anyway Thomas, can I give you a lift?"

"No thanks Stephen, I'm fine. See you tomorrow."

"God bless," smiled Stephen as he turned into the carpark.

Tom walked home alongside the gleaming Lagan which flowed softly under the summer sun, then through the spacious and tree-rich Ormeau Park to east Belfast.

He'd just arrived home from the Youth Club around nine thirty. It was late summer, and the nights had begun to lengthen. The family doctor knocked the door and proceeded to enter. He was a big bluff Ulsterman, and he was loved and revered throughout the community and beyond for his sacrificial service to people.

He nodded brusquely to Tom who rose quickly from the chair to greet him. "Come in Doctor Pitt."

He knew the way and made for the narrow stairs which he ascended awkwardly, armed with his battered medicine bag. Tom followed the doctor. His mother rose from her chair by the bedside. "Hello doctor. Would you like a cup of tea?"

"No, God bless you missus, but I haven't got a minute and "I have many miles to go before I sleep"."

She moved off and downstairs. Tom sat on the bed in his own room, the door was open. The doctor took the chair she had vacated.

"Well Harry; how the hell are you tonight?" he growled.

"I'm in training for the Belfast Marathon. What do ya think?" bantered Harry.

The doctor took out a little brown bottle from his bag, removed the sterile packaging from a syringe and began to draw up from the bottle.

"This will ease your pain Harry, and let you sleep."

"Doctor, I'm lying here. No good to man nor beast. It's going to happen anyway. Could ye not just give me more o' that stuff and give me a shove over the brink?"

"You're having a rough Gethsemane, Harry, I know. But I'm only a G.P. not God."

"You'd put a dog down if it was suffering wouldn't ye?"

"I would, but you're not a dog. You're a man, made in His image. The issues of life and death are with Him, not us. Now, give me your arm." He administered the painkiller.

"Who would have believed it would have come to this?" sighed harry

"We're all in the queue Harry. We're all in the queue."

The doctor quickly packed his bag. "I'll see you tomorrow night Harry. God bless." He nodded sympathetically to Tom, and noisily negotiated his descent to the living room. He talked briefly to Tom's mother, and took his leave into the street where his car was parked.

Tom sat on the edge of the bed. An invisible enemy was draining his father of life. An unclean ghoul gloated over vain human attempts to save him. He bent down and kissed his father's clammy forehead. "I love you dad," he whispered, but his father had drifted quickly off into a deep sleep, and was breathing heavily. He made his way downstairs and joined his mother in their mutual grief that seemed to slowly drip, drip, like water on a worn stone.

Her eyes were red from incessant crying and lack of sleep. She kept an all-night vigil at her husband's bedside, dozing in the chair. She had worked since she left school at fourteen, in the mills and factories. Her last job before retirement was in the 'Pram Factory' at the top of the Castlereagh Road, where she did twice the work of a man for half the wages. She had brought Tom up with a rough but steady hand, and was the real stability in his life through hard and turbulent times. She was the homemaker, the matriarch who always seemed to bring order from chaos.

"You take my bed tonight mum," Tom suggested. "You're done in."

"No son. You need the sleep. Go to college. I don't think it will be long now. The doctor said he'd be movin' him to the Marie Curie Hospice as soon as a bed becomes free. Oh Tom, I don't know what else to do."

She was standing at the mantelpiece in the middle of the living room. Tom put his arms around her and she quietly sobbed upon his shoulder.

"Mum, no-one could have done any more. Stop beating yourself up."

The door knocked, Tom slowly detached himself and opened it. There was Timmy, smiling. His eyes were alive with hope and expectation.

"How's the wee bird Tommy?" He had called every day to check on his little feathered friend's progress.

"He's doing fine Tommy. In fact, he flew out of his box today. Not far mind you. He seems to be healing."

"Can I see him?"

"Sure." The little boy followed Tom into the scullery. Tom flicked the switch and the place flooded with light. Timmy leaned over the box and spoke soothingly to the little bird. Then he stood up, "Thanks Tommy." and made his way out, buoyant and happy.

Tom and his mother smiled. "At least there's some light in the darkness," he commented. His mother sighed and nodded.

The following evening, as Tom strolled to Norman's place, birdsong filled the air from an abundance of trees and hedges. Couples sauntered nonchalantly, drinking in the scent of flowers and grass, and luxuriating in the pleasant warmth. Dogs on leads with lolling pink tongues sniffed from tree to tree, quickly lifting back legs to leave a canine calling card, before they were unceremoniously hauled away by their impatient owners. The scene was a sweeping tableau of urban domesticity.

The tomatoes were thriving wonderfully. The red swelling spheres promised an abundant harvest. Everything in the greenhouse was vital and alive, stretching upward towards the animating sun.

He retired that night before his mum. The doctor had left half an hour before and his father was enjoying a profound sleep. They had half watched television for a while when he stood up, kissed his mother lightly on the forehead and went to bed. An hour later, after spraying the downstairs rooms with air freshener, she too climbed wearily up the stairs to keep her faithful vigil over her dying husband.

Tom rose first the next morning. Wiping the sleep from his eyes, he filled the electric kettle and switched it on. He put the yellow plastic basin in the large Belfast sink and ran some hot water from the geyser onto it. He stripped to the waist and, after tempering the hot water with cold from the tap, he proceeded to wash his hair and torso; then applied some shaving cream, taken from a small wooden cupboard above the sink, when he noticed something small at the base of the backdoor which opened into the yard.

The feathered body of the sparrow lay on the linoleum covered scullery floor.

"What's wrong?" asked his mother looking over his shoulder.

"The wee bird's dead," gasped Tom incredulously.

"Oh no!" his mum cried. "It must have been the air freshener I sprayed in here last night."

"Ahh mum!" groaned Tom. "It choked the wee thing. It couldn't breathe. That's why his wee beak is up against the crack at the bottom of the door. Ahhh no!"

"I'm so sorry Tom, I didn't realise." His mum began to cry.

"I know mum." He held her close and some of the shaving cream clung to her grey hair.

"I just don't know what I'm going to say to Timmy."

"Don't tell him I did it," she sobbed, "It'll break his wee heart. Oh, I'm so sorry."

"OK mum," he comforted her.

They held each other in mourning for the tiny creature whose tragic sojourn among them had been so fleeting.

"This is the best crop of tomatoes I've ever had. What's your secret Tom?" exclaimed Norman. They were surrounded by burgeoning plants their vines heavy with bright red voluptuous fruit. Norman sported a tan, and looked rested and relaxed.

"Looks like you were in Spain not Scotland," remarked Tom.

"The weather was glorious. We had a wonderful time in the Highlands and Islands; back in the ancestral homelands."

"Haggis hunting in the Highlands, a dangerous sport," joked Tom.

"You should have seen the big hairy beast that got away. Scary! Anyway, it is good to be back again in the salubrious suburbs of Ballyhackamore."

"Ballysnackamore more like with all these restaurants opening," quipped Tom.

"Of course, you know what Ballyhackamore means?"

"Haven't a clue!" laughed Tom.

"It's from the Irish, Baile Chacamór. The townland of The Big Shit! It seems it was a coach stop. Human cargo was not the only thing to be discharged!" A delighted Norman, carefully holding an imaginary cup and saucer; his little finger sticking out, exaggeratedly said in a snobby high-pitched voice "The next time you're hob-nobbing with the crème de la crème in Ballyhackamore, you'll know where you're going young Thomas!"

"Charmed I'm sure," bowed Tom. "You know that's the first time I've laughed in weeks."

"God gives us two great releases; laughter and tears. How is your father Tom?"

"He's like an ol' withered leaf waiting for the death wind. Any time now Norman. Any time now."

Harry was taken by ambulance to the Marie Curie centre on the Knock Carriageway. The road took its name from the townland of Knock Colmcille, meaning the Hill of the Dove of the Church; a reference to the sixth century saint, Colmcille.

The hospice was a pleasant modern facility surrounded by hedges, trees and neat gardens. Inside was bright, hygienic and welcoming. The staff were charming and helpful.

Harry was allocated a spacious well-lit room with a beautiful view of the garden. After his father had settled and had painkillers administered, he gradually descended into a fitful sleep. They both left after the sister in charge urged Tom's mother to go home and sleep.

A taxi took them home. Timmy was waiting outside the front door.

"Can I see the wee bird Tommy? Is he well?"

Tom's mother hurriedly opened the front door with the key taken from her leather purse and went inside. Tom turned to Timmy. "I've got some bad news Timmy," he began. He saw disappointment where there had been hope in Timmy's big dark eyes. "The wee fella died last night son. I found him this morning."

"But he was doing well! You said so yourself Tommy," complained the boy.

"I know Timmy, but these things happen. His little heart must have failed. His breathing could have been affected." Tommy knew this was true, but not all the truth, and it made him feel uneasy.

Timmy slowly bowed his head and turned to walk away.

"It was nobody's fault Timmy. These things happen."

"OK Tommy," whispered Timmy as he wiped the tears from his eyes and moved into the gathering darkness.

Tom's sleep was troubled that night. A shifting kaleidoscope of images danced on the screen of his imagination. He saw the face of young Timmy. Hope had died like the frail body of the little bird he offered with both hands. His mother appeared, pale and drawn with tears trickling down her cheeks. Norman was laughing among the red and green of the tomatoes. His father walked him by the hand through narrow streets. He viewed the panoramic sweep of Belfast, Black Mountain, Divis, Cavehill and Knockagh. He saw the docks skirting the lough; cranes and gantries like great cathedrals towering above the light industrial mist, as the last rays of a dying sun drained from Lagan Basin. He was haunted by the images of his emaciated father with his sunken eyes and skeletal frame. He heard the distant thunder of industry, and lightening of welding torches; the far-off boom of hollow metal hulls and the high-pitched scream of grinders like tortured souls.

Iron on iron, metal on metal, steel on steel. Bang! Bang! Bang!

Tom leapt out of bed, stumbled as quickly as he could downstairs and opened up to a large uniformed constable who had been hammering at the door. He mumbled, awkward and embarrassed.

"I'm sorry. Your father has passed away, and we've been sent to take you to the hospice. We'll wait while you dress."

He toted a submachine gun, while the grey armoured Land Rover growled quietly at the door. It bore the scars of many bricks, bolts and petrol bombs, and filled the street with the smell of diesel.

His mother stood at the top of the stairs, her face full of anxiety and dread. They both quickly dressed and mounted the "Hotspur" from the back. Both doors closed behind them. Tom and his mother sat facing each other on leather padded benches. The officer took a seat at the rear of the transport. The armoured vehicle was not built for speed and the occupants swayed and rolled as it progressed slowly through the virtually deserted streets to the final destination – the hospice.

"I'm so sorry," the matron, a middle-aged lady dressed in a navy-blue skirt and blouse, condoled, "but your husband's condition deteriorated so dramatically, it took us all by surprise."

She led the way through the building. Most of the lights were out except those which burned strategically to avoid accidents. The atmosphere was sinister and sepulchral. She ushered them both into a dark room, heavy with the scent of antiseptic, and flicked a switch. The lights shone with bright intensity. The place was cold and clinical. A white slab bore a body draped in a white sheet. The matron, followed by Tom and his mother, went to one end of the slab and slowly uncovered the head and shoulders of the corpse. Tom's mother began to weep. She sobbed into her handkerchief, and as he put his arm gently around her, she cried more loudly into his shoulder.

He hardly recognised the body that had been his father. The cheeks were clapped in; the eyes were sunken in their sockets. The skin bore a white, yellowish pallor like the edges of an old newspaper. It was the first time he had been confronted personally with the death of a human being. To Tom, the sight was ghastly. He was appalled by the brutal finality of it all; the ruthless termination of existence. There was no comfort here, no solace; only the total disfigurement of death.

Sure, the under-takers and embalmers would set to work and make it more tolerable. The cosmetics would be applied and the body dressed in Sunday best, complete with shirt and tie. But nothing, nothing could mitigate the awe-inspiring terror of the void.

The matron, like a warm clucking hen, offered her condolences and sympathy. She led the way back to the reception area of the centre, and arranged for tea to be brought.

Even though they had accepted the inevitability of Harry's death, nevertheless they were both shocked and moved when Harry finally died. They discussed the funeral arrangements half-heartedly, and slowly drank their tea. Eventually matron 'phoned for a taxi.

Tom sauntered out of the building deep in thought, a cocktail of emotions swirling in his being. The sun was firing the tops of the trees on the eastern hills. He could smell the freshness of dew-soaked grass and hedges. The dawn chorus began to increase in volume, filling the summer morning with vitality and joy.

Then he spied it and smiled. A spritely little sparrow earnestly seeking his breakfast, hopped gingerly over the green grass and melted into the undergrowth.

Brian Ervine was born and bred in the heart of working-class east Belfast, and has lived there all his life maintaining strong links with the community working through local churches, as a politician and as a school teacher. He graduated with a degree in Education from Queen's University Belfast, later returning to complete a further degree in  Theology. His plays, including 'Somme Day Mourning', have been produced at the MAC and other venues throughout Belfast; and he has performed his own songs in such arenas as the Great Hall in Stormont. Now retired, Brian continues to actively research, write and perform.

Brian Ervine C/o
Skainos Square,
239 Newtownards Road,
Belfast BT4 1AF

Email: brianervine1951@gmail.com